Rania Hanna is a Syrian–American neuroscience doctoral student at Geor. *Daughter* is her debut novel. She lives in Northern Virginia.

T0013927

The Jinn Daughter

Rania Hanna

hoopoe

AN IMPRINT OF AUC PRESS

First published in 2024 by
Hoopoe
113 Sharia Kasr el Aini, Cairo, Egypt
420 Lexington Avenue, Suite 1644, New York, NY 10170
www.hoopoefiction.com

Hoopoe is an imprint of The American University in Cairo Press
www.aucpress.com

ISBN 978 1 649 03363 5

Library of Congress Cataloging-in-Publication Data applied for

1 2 3 4 5   28 27 26 25 24

Designed by Adam el-Sehemy

For Tita Lilly, our matriarch.

1

THE DEAD HAVE BEEN DROPPING ALL night.

I wake before the sun is bright enough to cut across the horizon and I gather the pomegranate seeds scattered in front of my home—bright fruit that collects like a crimson puddle under the twisted tree. There are many seeds this morning, and the weight of the basket tilts me as I hobble back inside my cottage.

My daughter, Layala, is still sleeping in her cot as I sit down, joints clicking. I am only thirty, yet the years weigh heavier on me than they should, and I sigh as I pluck seeds out of the basket. They're red and plump, these seeds, and leave my hands sticky. I press them between two pieces of wood and let the juice seep into a bowl. Each seed is a soul's story, and every story must be told. As *Hakawati Jinn*, it is my duty to tell the stories of the dead and send the souls to final—and hopefully, peaceful—death.

When the seeds have been pressed into a ruby juice, I take a sip and wrinkle my nose. "Bitter today," I mutter to myself, pouring honey into the cup. I stir, then take another drink.

The stories come in flashes, too quick for my mind to understand, and I'm too tired to try, but my magic is fast enough to catch them.

Snatches of a river flowing fast; the brown of a head topped with seaweed, floating on.

I catch the green of a tree and a swing hanging from a thick branch. I think I hear the growl of a bear. Or the clash of blades. But everything comes too fast, and there are so many stories to tell: stories of days and lives lived. I rarely ever see the last moments of death, thankfully.

My fingers bend and scrawl, weaving stories in the air. The words leave my fingers, curling into smoke. I drink more of the juice, weaving the smoky tales in the air with my other hand. The stories disappear almost as soon as they form, swallowed back into death.

Layala stirs, slipping out of her bed and padding around behind me in the kitchen. She says nothing as she sets a pot of tea to boil and begins making our breakfast.

I drink the last of the juice and, more out of habit than need, glance at the lone pomegranate seed I keep in a small glass jar on a shelf.

Layala's father.

Those who have died by their own hand have no place in Mote. They are banished to Jahannam, to suffer eternal cold and perpetual executions. Preserving his soul seed was the only love I could show him after his death, to keep him in the Waiting Place of death rather than write his tale and send him to suffer.

He visits us sometimes, as happy as any dead could be.

As if thinking it conjures him, he ghosts into the cottage, his body more smoke and ash than flesh and blood.

"Illyas," I say, rising to my feet.

He bends to kiss me, soft and, if not warm, then not the cold expected with the dead. And though his face fades through mine, I pretend I feel his solid flesh. "Always beautiful, Nadine," he says, and his smile is sad.

"*Sabah al-khair*, baba," our daughter greets, throwing her arms through the air as if to hug him. *Good morning, father.*

He can only keep his form a few minutes in a day, in the moments when the sun's light turns from red and orange to its bright day colors.

"And how are my girls today?" he asks, as he does every visit.

"Good," Layala says. "I'm going to see *jido* again today."

My dead lover's face stiffens at the mention of his father, but he forces a smile onto his face. "You should spend more time at home, with your mother," he says, and I throw him a grateful look.

But before Layala can respond, Illyas disappears, as the sun's light breaks through our windows and the morning is fully awake.

We both sigh, always wishing for just one more minute with him.

"I wish we could go into death," Layala says. "You're a jinn; you're made of death itself. Are you sure there's no way—"

"No, Layl. I've told you before. Jinns manage death; they don't enter it or keep its company, not if they can help it." I bite the tip of my tongue, tasting the lie that is far more bitter than the seeds I drank. *You lie to keep her safe, to keep her from asking too many questions.*

I hate lying to my daughter's face, but her questions have plagued me for years. Ever since she was a child, she wanted to know: What was death like? Was it something you could take trips to? Could she visit it? What about the souls who don't pass, could they be her friends? What magic did she have, being my daughter? Did she have jinn magic, too? Was there no way?

It's better she knows as little as possible, even if she is half-jinn. She'll likely never have my magic, and it's best she doesn't.

"I'm going to jido's," she says to me. "I'll be gone all day."

"Your father is right, you know. You should stay home more, learn a craft so you can support yourself when I die."

"You'll be around for many more years, maman. You just don't like jido much," she teases, kissing me on my head as she darts off to get dressed. "Besides, his garden needs work. The trees aren't as tall as they should be, and the vines are choking them." She flashes me a bright smile as she flutters through the house.

3

I glance back at that lone pomegranate seed on the shelf. *He's nothing like his father, and thank the heavens for that.*

My daughter leaves the house in a flurry of color and voice. "Bye, maman!" she yells, barely throwing me a parting look. I give her enough time until she's out of sight, then pull an empty bottle from a shelf, another one filled with honey, and a canteen of water.

I take the stony pathway at the back of the house and head straight for the cemetery. It's filled with chipped tombstones wearing moss shoulders and spiderwebs. No flowers or notes mark any grave anymore; the cemetery has long been forgotten. Which is why it's perfect for my escapes into death. I lean back against a tree and spy a fox watching me. The burbling stream beyond chuckles, far enough away that I don't see it through the thick tree branches, but close enough that I hear it and smell how cold it is. It is fed by death, with waters that run silver at night and gold in the morning. The same waters I keep Illyas's seed in to keep it from rotting.

The fox cocks its head at me, his snout curled up in a characteristic smile. "Come to see me walk into death, little one?" I ask. It dashes off, bushy tail hanging low.

I fill the empty jar with dirt from a grave, mix in the honey and water, and drink. My mouth fills with granules of stone and sand, and I try not to chew any, only swallow. The honey does little to mask the taste, but it'll do.

While the dirt water sloshes in my stomach and I feel the weight of stones settle in me, I press my hands to the ground and let the cold of the earth seep into my skin. It's familiar, this feeling of being one foot in the warmth of life and the other in the cold of death. I feel comforted, just as I did when I sat in my own maman's lap as a child, as she told me the stories of our people and the magic running in our veins.

Lightning strikes through me, a jolt to my body as I enter death. And Illyas is there to greet me, as he always does. He's a shadow first, then the smoke curls in around him and I can just make out his features. He's smiling, as usual, his hand out-stretched. I pretend to take it, though my hand goes through his.

"Hakawati," he says, calling me by my title rather than my name. "*Hiyati.*" *My life.*

It's pale in death, any color so watered down it's more an insult to the color it mimics. There are trees, though, pale green leaves with bark the color of faded animal hide. And the sky is so muted, I'm never sure whether it's blue or gray or a dirty white.

"Illyas," I say, letting him guide me to a bench. Death surprisingly has small comforts for those who can't or won't pass on to Mote or Jahannam. "How are you?"

He laughs, the sound gravelly but warm, like honey mixed with crushed spices. I want to hold him like he used to hold me when he was alive. But bodies move and fit differently in death, less flesh and more ash. "As good as can be. And you?" He leans close and reaches a hand out, as if to brush the hair off my forehead. I don't feel his skin, but there's still a trail of warmth. I want to lean my cheek into his touch, to rest my weight against him.

"Well enough. Your daughter threw animal shit at some boys who were bothering her yesterday. I don't know if I should encourage her fiery personality or douse it," I say, laughing.

Illyas chuckles, but there's a tightness in his face. "She should be careful," he says. "She's still your daughter, and they don't take kindly to that." He brushes a hand across my face again, and I pretend I can still grasp his scent.

"There's so much I want to tell her," I admit, "but I don't know if I should. And I've told her so many lies over the years. How do I undo that?"

He says nothing, and when I try to move in closer to his chest, we fade into each other, smoke curling into smoke. We pull back, our bodies regaining substance. It's as if we repel each other, our skin, our bodies refusing to meld the way they did when Illyas was alive. I swallow a scream of frustration.

At least you can see him, talk to him, even if you can't touch him or smell him.

"Hakawati, tell her a story," Illyas says, interrupting my thoughts. "You've spun her tales since she was in the cradle; she will *feel* your meaning, even if she doesn't understand it. Weave her a story and see what she says."

"She'll roll her eyes and ask to go to her grandfather's house. She has little patience for me lately."

He shakes his head. "She reminds me of me when I was her age. I don't know if that's a good thing."

"I loved you at that age," I say, reaching out for his hand. I let mine hover over his so we feel each other's warmth.

"*Loved?*" he echoes, smirking. "Not anymore?"

I crack a smile. "You know you're my one and true love."

He smiles wide, but then his expression sobers. "You shouldn't be alone anymore. Layl is getting older. She will one day leave home to start her own. What will you do then?"

"Visit you more often."

Illyas huffs at that. "You should find someone. You should," he repeats when I twist my face up in a "no."

"I remember you being rather jealous of a certain Ihab in the village," I tease, "when he gave me flowers during the midsummer festival."

His sudden bark of a laugh spears through my heart. "I was young. And I seem to recall you encouraging him, just to make me jealous."

"I might have," I say with a smile. "I don't remember."

"Lies. You remember everything." The lines around his eyes crinkle, as if he were still made of true flesh. I want to hold him, feel him, skin on skin. Instead, I get to my feet and try to numb the raw pain in my chest.

"I should return. The sun will be setting soon." Time works differently in death than in life, at once faster and slower. I already feel sluggish, the effects of death tugging at my soul, trying to pull it from my body and claim it.

"I'll walk you home," he says, and we both smile, because there's no leaving death for Illyas tonight, not until the sun wakes up in life and he can steal away for a few minutes.

I hover my lips at his cheek in the mimicry of a kiss.

"Goodbye, Hakawati," he says. "I'll miss you until next time."

2

LAYALA SLIPS INTO THE HOUSE that night far later than she's allowed to be out. The door clicks shut behind her, and I hear her slip off her soft leather boots and set them by the fire. She hangs her coat up on the nail by the door and undoes her long braid.

"Maman?" she whispers. I pretend to be asleep but watch her through my slitted eyes as I lay in my cot. A smile beams on her face, one that stops my heart for a breath. It's the smile of a young girl in love.

I want to reach out to her, to tell her that love will come, more mature love, and to wait. But I know it'll be no use; I had that love at her age. Who am I to begrudge her it?

Instead, I let her be and stay up the rest of the night, counting my prayer beads and asking a wish-prayer on each one.

Keep her safe.
Keep her happy.
Let her find good love.
Let her know peace.
Let her know her heart and mind.
Let her be.

It's a prayer I've said for Layala since before she was born, when all I knew of her were her strong legs and fists inside my womb.

I fall asleep, waking every hour, my heart stammering in my chest. I keep checking that Layala is in her cot, but every time I look, her chest rises and falls in the way only a peaceful sleeper knows.

But before the sun has even had a chance to yawn, she is up and about, setting tea, kneading dough, and laying out the *za'atar* and *zayt* we will eat for breakfast.

"Layl, you're up early," I say.

"Sabah al-khair, maman."

"Your father won't be here for another two hours, at least," I add.

She ignores me, humming and smiling to herself. A question hovers on my lips—who is the boy? I want to know, but I don't ask her. Let her tell me in her own time.

She sits at the table, scripting something on empty sheets of cream paper.

"What are you writing?" I ask, forcing myself not to lean over and read it myself.

"Stories. Like you do, except on paper instead of in the air." She flashes me a smile and dips her head back to write some more.

"Your stories and mine are different, *binti*," I tell her. *My daughter.*

She rolls her eyes in all the exasperation of a girl on the cusp of womanhood. Still, she's just fourteen, and I pull her in for a hug. She smells the same as she did when she was a baby—of powder and sweet skin. I breathe in her scent, keeping her in my arms for as long as she'll let me. But soon enough, she's unwrapping herself from my embrace.

"What did you do yesterday?" I ask, unable to help myself. "At jido's." I notice then the knees of her pants, stained with dirt. She didn't change out of them last night.

"Were you in the cemetery again?" I ask, staring pointedly at the evidence.

She's pulled out two dried flowers from her pocket now. They're laid like corpses on the table, but Layala soon cups them in her palms, as if trying to warm them.

"I don't see why you hate me being around buried bodies so old they're dust when you're always spending time with *souls*." She doesn't look up from her writing.

"It's my job."

"I went into town," she says finally. I notice she hasn't answered my question.

"Again? To throw more horse shit at the town boys?"

She cracks a smile but shakes her head. "Just to walk."

I'm watching the flowers, now less pale than before, more colorful, like a child's pale cheeks turning pink in the cold.

"Mmm, knowing you, you may have said a few words, too. Words to the wrong person, at the wrong time."

She sighs and glances up at me. "I saw the blacksmith's apprentice and his friends and may have exchanged a few words with them."

It's my turn to sigh. "What kind of words, Layl?" I try to force the strain out of my voice.

"They called me witch and death-bringer. Jinn's daughter. Soul eater." She frowns. "They tell me I'm made of sin, maman." Her voice fades at the end and she turns her head away.

"Layl," I start, tucking a tangled curl behind her ear. I force a gentleness into my voice. "Layl, how many times have I told you, you walk away when people say—"

Her face screws up in anger and she pulls away from me, the curl untucking itself again. "That blacksmith boy deserved it. I only told him what I thought of them."

"Yes, but their parents might now come to our house, and what good would that do for us?"

"They have no right!"

"Many people have no right to say or do the things they do, but the difference is, some get away with it, and some don't. We're in the second group, Layl."

I scrape the chair back against the old wooden floor harder than I mean to, then set down a bowl of herbs on the table in front of her.

Layala sighs and pushes aside her flowers, then reaches out to pick at the herbs, ripping off leaves and tossing the stems aside. "It's not fair," she says after a while. "And it's not fair you're stuck all the way out here, just because the towns-people needed a hakawati to deal with their dead."

I don't say anything, only cut potatoes into blocks and dump them into a bowl of oil. Layala takes the bowl and rubs in the herbs, releasing fragrance into our small cottage. Soon, we have a fire growing against the cold of the morning and food cooking over it. The air is thick with strong herbs, but thicker in the strained silence between us.

"I wish . . ." she starts to say when we've eaten and she's already moving about our house, pulling things off shelves and out of drawers. I notice how long her limbs are, how much bigger she fits into our one room cottage, like she's outgrowing it far faster than she should. Even her cot, which suited her fine just a year ago, seems almost too short for her growing figure.

And then I wonder, *is she outgrowing* me, *too?*

My daughter doesn't finish her sentence, only shakes her head and sits back in her chair, arms folded over her chest.

"I have wishes, too," I whisper. "But they never come true."

3

"OFF TO JIDO'S?" I ASK, as Layala slips on her velvety blue robe. It's the one she keeps for special occasions, though we rarely have those.

When was the last time we did anything special, except for her birthday? No wonder she spends more time outside our home than she does in it.

Layala nods, but her cheeks flush red with the lie. Perhaps I should send a hawk out to follow her. I decide I will. Just to make sure she's safe.

As soon as she dashes out the door, barely a goodbye on her lips, I take a clay ochre-hued hawk from the shelf and run my hands over it. The clay is cool and smooth, but as I slide my fingers down the hawk's back, the clay grows warm and quivers in my palm.

The clay hawk's eyes flash open, and I set it down on the table, letting it grow to full size.

"Watch over my girl, Saqr," I tell it, weaving the words in the air with my fingers and letting them sink into the hawk's soft, downy feathers.

Saqr's eyes glint, and in the next breath he's out the door and streaking into the sky.

I grab my basket and go outside to gather the pomegranate seeds from the night before. The basket is heavy this morning, though there are fewer seeds than normal. Just some handfuls of dead souls. But as I carry the basket on my hip, my bones feel weighed down. I glance around to make sure

I didn't miss any of those unmistakable red seeds. To leave a seed behind is to delay a soul's passage through death.

Satisfied I've gathered everything, I turn toward the house, passing by the rows of ghoulsbane Layala planted to ward off any stray ghouls passing my way. The air smells sweet, too, of lavender and honeymoss, of rose petals and everything else Layala planted over the years. Things she brought back to life, even when they were on the verge of dying.

Perhaps, perhaps she has magic in her after all . . .

I shake my head of the thought. *She is human, not magic, only blood and flesh and bone.*

But remember when she brought home a sapling that was so brown and dry it crumbled when you touched it? And she brought it back to life in three days?

I glance up at that sapling, now a tree standing sentry beside my cottage.

It wanted to live, like all life. Layala has no magic. And it is best she doesn't.

But the thought feels wrong, weak, and I know—I *know*—it isn't true.

Once inside my home, I shut the door behind me. My body feels slow, and my knees click as I sit down. Even my eyelids feel heavy, and I blink a few times, trying to keep my eyes from going dry. But being tired is no excuse, so I press the seeds into a juice, and I drink.

Every morning of every day for fourteen years, I've done this. Every soul that has died on this side of the ocean, in the towns stretching further than I've ever been or ever will be, I've helped pass on.

The stories today are sharp, cutting through me like daggers. I pour extra honey, stirring it in until I can no longer taste tart pomegranate, only the cloying sweetness of the fresh honey I bought just days ago from the market, and the surly lady who sold it to me. I paid double the coin for it than the villagers, I know, but the color was so rich I couldn't resist.

"Jinn," the woman said like a curse as she passed me the jar, pursing her lips in such a way I thought she was going to spit on me. But she turned her glance away from me, taking care not to touch me as I took the jar from her.

Back in my hut, in the middle of weaving the dead's tales, I catch the tail of one story, and it surprises me. I know this woman, an old one from the village next door. She used to cook for my family when we were wealthy and jinns were respected. In the days when I was young and the world was fresh to me. A time that feels like generations ago but is barely three decades old. Like every other soul, her story is told through images, through symbols that make little sense, even when stitched together. But every soul has its own tale, and so the images of this woman's life sharpen into the story of a pearl tree.

I *feel* the story, as if I'm living it myself, and I'm transported into a small garden—though I'm still in my own kitchen—and find a man standing in it.

The pearl tree stood alone in the center of a poor man's garden.

It dropped iridescent pearls every morning, but if the man got too close, branches whipped out to slap him. Pearls at his feet, and not one to sell in the markets.

Still, the man tried every so often to snatch just one pearl. But each effort left him with a welt across the face and a gash on his arm.

One day, the man grew so angry he decided to cut down the tree. He took an axe to its roots, dashed them into pieces, and gathered the pearls. One basket, two, then three were filled.

The tree lay in ruin, its once proud trunk a stump in the garden. Its branches lay scattered about, hacked into pieces.

The man smiled to himself, thinking of all the riches he would buy. New teeth to replace the ones he had sold for a bit of coin to buy his food. New shoes to protect his rough bare feet from being cut on stones along the road. A new house with a roof that didn't leak. And, most of all, a wife. A beautiful one, to be dressed in jewels and dresses fit for a rani.

But when the man checked on his baskets later in the day, he found nothing but ash. He pulled at his thin hair, ripping it out in clumps. Then he ran back into his house to cry.

And in the midst of his bawling, a knock sounded at his door.

He snatched the door open, finding the kingdom's prince standing there.

"I have heard tales of a magic tree that drops pearls instead of leaves. Do you know of this tree?"

"Why do you ask?" said the man.

"I wish to plant it in my own gardens. I will pay handsomely for it."

The old man glanced behind the prince, at the severed pieces of the pearl tree.

"You did this?" the prince said, following his gaze.

The man nodded, tears again welling up in his eyes.

"Stupid, stupid man," the prince said. "Do you know what you've done? That tree, those pearls, they are the dead. The souls of our dead. Without that tree, the dead cannot pass to the next life. They will become ghouls, wandering the earth, wreaking havoc on it."

And just as the man had hacked at the tree, the prince's soldiers cut down the man and left him behind to rot. They gathered the pieces of the tree, hoping upon hope that there was some magic in the world that could heal it.

The story ends there, and I am none the wiser to its meaning. Still, I sense the woman clutching her story to her breast, worth more to her than gold to the living. Her dead spirit understands the tale more than my living one could. I sense her gratitude, like the sun's warmth on a cold winter day, and then I feel the thread between us cut.

"*Rohik ma'eek,*" I whisper. *Your soul be with you.* She's paid her way into Mote with the tale; she will have everlasting peace.

I turn back to my juice and drink the rest, weaving each story as lovingly as I can. The morning spreads apart into the afternoon before I am finished. Night falls, and still Layala hasn't returned home. She's never done this before, made a habit of coming home late, and panic stirs in my heart, in my belly. I feel as if I've swallowed stones and they've settled in my stomach, weighing me down.

Saqr? I think. *Where is she?* I pad over to the door, sticking my head outside. I glance expectantly at the stony pathway to our house, hoping to find Layala on it. But it's empty save for a rabbit who hops away into the woods beyond. My breath is ragged now, and then I see a familiar streak in the sky.

Saqr shoots in past me through the door, landing deftly on the table.

"Tell me," I demand, laying my hand lightly on his back. My mind links with Saqr's. I see flashes of Layl as Saqr followed her. She walks through town, her velvet hood up to hide her face. *Smart girl.*

She walks into a ribbon shop, then out, leaving empty-handed. She wanders more around town, looking at the wares, her face always hidden from others' eyes. Villagers mill past her, stopping at stalls, exchanging coins for goods as wares are bought and sold.

Until she stops at the edge of the market, and instead of turning back home, she continues on. She walks to the village over, her steps growing lighter, more skips than steps now. She's happy.

Happier than I've seen her in a while, I realize.

And then she stops at a door, glancing around before she knocks, once, twice. The door swings open. I see a hand, pale with long fingers, grip my daughter's arm and pull her in.

Saqr's view shifts, now glancing through the window of the house. Layala is inside, sitting by a fire, her cloak off. Her face is in full view of a boy. Just as I expected.

But this is no ordinary boy. He is one made of smoke, hair tipped with flames. His face is pale, his eyes dark, and his teeth shine with silver. He is no ordinary boy, for he is a jinn.

And some jinns are trouble.

4

IT'S MORNING. I PACE MY one-room house, waiting for my daughter to return. But she doesn't.

Go fetch her, I think. *But then she'll know you're spying on her.*

No! You are the mother, not her; you decide what she does.

And in another thought, I think, *leave her be. She will tell you all when she is ready. Trust your child.*

And so, I let her be, for now. But I have a mother's worry flowing through my veins, so I awaken the hawk once more.

"Saqr," I say, "Go find Layala."

The hawk leaves, and I continue my pacing. Do I walk to the next village? Leave our cottage at the edge of the woods and search for my child? Or do I trust she will make good decisions?

Didn't you make horrible, stupid decisions when you were just a bit older than her?

Saqr returns a while later, and I lay a hand on him. The images come in snatches, as if he darted around, looking for a better vantage point.

She's asleep, her cloak draped over her fully clothed body, the fire burning bright.

So, Layala spent the night at the jinn boy's house.

The jinn sits in his chair, watching her, stoking the flames of a fire every so often to keep it from burning too low. I narrow my eyes at him, even though I'm only seeing him through Saqr's memory.

Saqr picks up a stick and flings it at the window, then hides from view. He perches on a tree branch, looking into the house. Layala stirs, then notices the morning light shining through the window.

I can't hear what she says, but I see her lips move. Her eyes are wide and she's shaking off the jinn's grasp on her arm.

I think I see her mouth 'I have to go.'

Saqr's memory cuts off then, and a breath later, his body is quivering, hardening, and he is clay again. I set him up on his shelf and go outside to gather the morning's seeds.

I'm sitting at my table, drinking pomegranate juice, when Layala rushes in through the door.

"I was worried all night," I tell her, my voice calm, even though I note a little shakiness to it. I pull up a chair and pat it, inviting her to sit.

She remains on her feet. "I fell asleep at jido's," she lies, not meeting my gaze.

"I see. Did you eat yet?"

She shakes her head, now picking at the edge of our small wooden table. "I'm going to rest," she says.

"I thought you slept at your grandfather's?" I put a hand to her head, as if feeling for fever. "Are you unwell?"

"No, just tired," she mutters, and her cheeks flush red. I let her go; best to not press her and have her shut herself off from me.

No, let her come to me with her heart's secrets in her own time.

Layala undresses and slips into bed, facing away from me. I bend over her, tucking the covers under her chin and around her slender body, just as I did when she was younger.

"I love you, maman," she says, whispering into her pillow. "I'll never do anything to hurt you."

I'm surprised by this, but only kiss her soft cheek, still round with baby fat yet to shed. "I know, hiyati."

I stoke the fire to make sure she's warm, then slip outside. The air is cold, and I wrap my maman's old cloak tight around me. I long for the feel of the warm earth under me, for Illyas's smile, for his reassuring words.

I make a snap decision and steal back into the house, taking jars and water, before padding toward the cemetery and back into death.

Illyas finds me, as usual.

"Hiyati," he says, "what's wrong?" His brows are furrowed as he tries to draw me close, but our bodies aren't flesh enough for that. Instead, he leads me to a crumbling tower and has me sit down. The pale ground is made of tiles, cracked and cool, flowers and weeds growing through the cracks. Death mimics life, but it's never the same.

"It feels strange here," I note, glancing around. Even death has movement, but it's still—too still—and it's missing the *something* that gives it a semblance of life.

"It's new," Illyas agrees. "A few of the others stuck here wanted to build a town." He shrugs, but he's still watching me with worry deep in his eyes. We are in . . . I'm not sure what, but it's a town, more a village, and it's beautiful, at least for death.

I eye the gate circling the town and the fence it's attached to. Both stand three heads higher than I am tall. It's been years since Illyas and I broke into places we shouldn't be in, giggling from the thrill of chasing each other into ramshackle houses and walled-up gardens.

I glance around, expecting to see huts thrown together, built out of what the land gave and what could be gathered in the woods and tied or nailed together with scraps. Instead, the houses are in neat rows, gardens and trees planted in sections of raised earth. Vines grow on the houses' stone walls, a neat cloak protecting the stone from being bleached by rain and sun. The faint scent of jasmine wafts over me.

I scan for movement, but the town is as still as an empty grave. Stiller even, because even graves have crawling worms.

Despite the beauty, the town *feels* dead. Nothing stirs, not a leaf, not the grass, not a curtain behind an open window. There's a layer of dust on everything, as if the town were abandoned. Or frozen in time.

It reminds me of the glass globe filled with little specks suspended in water that Layala's jido, Abu Illyas, gave her when she was much younger. She would shake the globe, watching the little white specks settle on the miniature village set inside the sphere. Then she would shake it again, laughing as her head bounced back and forth. I smile at the memory, at how a simple little toy could bring her so much joy.

There's nothing sentient around that I can see. Not a lone rabbit nibbling on a plant or a bird resting on a branch.

I shake my head of my thoughts and memories. "She's in love with a jinn boy," I say.

"Who? Layala?" he says, his eyebrows furrowing deeper.

I nod. "I saw them, through Saqr. She spent the night with the boy."

He tenses.

"She kept her clothes," I add quickly, but it does little to ease the tension rippling through his body. "But she lied to me."

"Who's the boy?" he asked, his voice gruffer than I've heard it in a while.

"I don't know. But I'll find out."

Illyas gives a sharp nod, his frown carved as though in stone. "I'll wring his neck if he does anything to hurt her."

I snort. "You and me both, hiyati. The last thing I'd want is for her to fall pregnant at barely fifteen."

Both our faces flush; our second-greatest mistake, and greatest joy, has been Layala. Born to young parents who knew nothing of the world, never mind raising a child, Layala tore out of me, bright red and screaming, on a night just shy of my sixteenth birthday. Illyas was three years older and he fainted at all the blood. I remember cleaning my daughter's face of my insides while fanning him with a slip of paper.

Illyas reaches over to hover his lips over mine, and for a moment, I feel a memory of his warmth. Then it is snatched away, and lightning strikes through my body.

Something is pulling my soul back into my body.

I gulp in harsh, cold air and flick my eyes open, only to find my daughter standing before me. Her face is twisted in anger, her hands planted firmly on her hips.

"Maman," she says, and it sounds like she's accusing me of something. "What are you doing?"

I sniff and get to my feet, dusting dirt off me. "I needed some fresh air," I say. "I guess I fell asleep." I realize the sun is setting now, the air much colder than before.

She narrows her eyes at me, as if not quite believing what I say. "I woke up and you weren't there," she accuses. "I waited, thinking you went for a walk, but you never came back."

Her gaze lands on a clump of drooping flowers near a gravestone, and she reaches out for them. Her hands hover over the petals, and slowly, slowly, the stems straighten.

No. Please, no. Let her not have an ounce of magic in her veins. Let her live a long, normal life.

"Well," I say, reaching my hand out so she can help me up, distracting her. The flower wilts again, and Layala turns to me. I grunt, heaving my weight forward to stand. "Long day, I suppose. Help your maman to the house, then," I add, leaning on her strong young figure. Going into death wears the body out more than I like to admit to myself.

Back in the house, I set a kettle to boil, not tired enough to sleep. Layala sits beside me, legs curled under her. She picks at her nails, a habit she has only when something is on her mind. The air is thick with herbs and the scent of rose petals, all picked from our garden.

Layala has been planting more, buying seedlings from the market and growing on every inch of earth she can around the house. I smile as a memory washes over me.

"What is your favorite color, Layaloon?"

She was three, almost four years old, and she was always playing in the dirt, in the grass, whispering to the wildflowers growing between our home and the woods.

"*Green, maman,*" *she said, laughing, one tooth in the front loose.* "*Green like the grass.*"

"*Green?*" *I repeat, picking her up and throwing her up in the air.* "*Not blue like the sky? Or yellow like the sun?*"

"*Maman!*" *she giggled.* "*Green, green, green! Green because I made the grass go brown to green,*" *she said in her high child's voice.*

I set her down, my blood running cold. "*What do you mean Layl? Brown to green?*"

She takes my hand in her tiny one and leads me to a patch of dry grass under the shade of a tall and wide tree. She points at a tiny spot of green in the middle of all that brown. "*Green,*" *she says.* "*I made it green.*"

"What is it, *kushtbani?*" I use her father's nickname for her: *thimble.* She was so tiny when she was born, she could fit into the palm of his hand if curled up.

"Nothing, maman," she says with a sigh. "I just . . . I want to tell you something, but not now."

She looks at me with her wide, dark eyes, eyelashes fringing them like tassels on a curtain.

"Tell me when you're ready, kushtbani. I can wait."

My heart aches at her beauty as she smiles at me. She doesn't see it yet, but under those baby cheeks are a grown woman's bones.

She pushes back her chair and steps over to her cot, and though she is just feet away from me, I've never felt further from my child. There are too many lies between us, and I must do something about it.

Night falls, and the next morning comes angry, with rain pelting the window, the wind howling through the trees.

I dash outside, gathering as many seeds as I can. Layala helps, grabbing handfuls of pomegranate and dirt and grass and shoving them into the basket. We run back inside, laughing at the downpour as we peel off our sodden clothing.

"I'll get the fire going, maman."

I sit down and sift through the seeds, setting aside the clumps of grass Layala grabbed. I juice the seeds, taking a sip to taste the mood. A sense of sadness washes over me, and I swallow the urge to cry.

"Is everything fine, maman?"

I nod, reaching for a lemon.

"Ah," Layl says. "It's sad seeds."

"Very," I say, squeezing the lemon into the juice and stirring. The sourness of the lemon masks the sadness of the souls, enough that I can drink without sobbing.

The stories shove around in my mind, snatches of sound, morsels of flavor. I get the whiff of warm cinnamon, the taste of cardamom in rice. The feel of a baby's skin, the weight of a warm fur around a neck on a cold winter day.

The stories clamor for my attention, each one trying to be the next that gets written. Souls can be impatient, eager to move on. Eager to have their tale written to pay Mote, the final gatekeeper of death.

I try my best, the ache in my bones growing and the din in my head rising. A headache is coming on.

I sense Layala near me, then feel the press of a cloth to my nose. I must be bleeding again, the strain of storytelling too much.

"Maman," she says, her voice sounding far away. "Take a break. The dead can wait."

"No rest for the dead," I insist, barely aware of what I'm saying. "No rest for the weary."

A story floats toward me. I feel its incessant nagging, a whining sound that builds in my ears like the church bell in town on a Sunday morning.

A young man spent his days drinking and casting lots at the gambling tables. Every morning, he stumbled home and

25

his poor father helped him to bed. The son would have vomit encrusted in his clothes, and his hair would be covered in sweat and dirt.

Fed up with his son, one day, the father tells him, "*Ibni*,"— my son—"how about you spend just this one night without getting sakran? Spend one night without drink."

The son laughs, then says to his father, "Baba, for you, I will do as you say. Just this one night."

The father considers this. "Come," he says. "Take me to the place you like the most for drink. We will watch, and I will show you what I see."

The two go to the son's favorite tavern and walk inside. Men sit in chairs, slumped over from drink or arguing with each other in slurred words.

The son glances around and spots his friends, but he keeps to the shadows, watching them instead.

"See?" says the father. "This is what I see when you are sakran: a foolish man who can't even string two sensible words together and who stumbles around like a babe just learning to walk."

They stay another hour, when the drunken men begin fighting over quibbles or vomiting over each other. The son is disgusted and turns his face away from the tavern.

"Baba," he admits, "you are right. I will mend my ways immediately."

But his father is not so easily placated. "Ibni," he says, "do one more thing for me. Go, go find the King of Gamblers, and see how he lives."

The son grins and seeks out this King. He searches through villages and towns, asking for where the King of Gamblers resides.

The first old man he meets tells him to seek a shaman in the village over. He will know where the King is.

The son goes to the shaman, who tells him to seek an old goatherd who dwells in the valley. The son finds the

26

goatherd, who tells him to find the medicine woman who lives in the forest.

The son finds the medicine woman, who tells him, "Ah, ibni, I know the one you seek. He is my brother, and he lives just up that mountain." She points at the mountain in the distance. "Climb the mountain, and there you will find the King of Gamblers."

The son spends days reaching the mountain. And more days climbing it. He stops at the first person he sees.

It is an old man with skin like leather and teeth stained with tobacco.

"I want to meet the King of Gamblers," the son says.

The man looks at him and invites him into the simple tent he lives in. The son enters, finding a threadbare carpet laid on the ground and a rolled mat in the corner. There is no food but a bit of bread with green mold, and nothing to drink but a pot of tea.

The old man offers his food and drink, but the son refuses and offers his own food instead.

The man tears greedily into the dried meats and figs the son has with him, then leans back to watch him.

Then he says, "Why do you seek the King of Gamblers?"

"My father, he told me to search for him."

"Ah," the old man says. "Well, you have found him."

The son flicks his eyes around him. The palace he expected to find is but a tattered tent. The riches, the women, the feasts he sought—he found none.

"Now I know why my father told me to find you," the son says. "For the King of Gamblers is no king at all."

I write the story and, as the last word is set, the soul snatches its tale and I am left with just the sour taste of the lemons.

Just as I turn to my daughter, an angry knock sounds at the door. We never have visitors.

I want to ignore the door and keep the curtains closed tight, but the knocking continues.

"Get behind me," I tell her as I slip out of my chair and grab a wooden spoon from the table.

The knocks are angrier, and so are the voices behind the door.

"Open, Hakawati!"

"Layl, go through the roof," I say, meaning the short ladder that leads to the flat top of our cottage.

"No, maman."

This is no time for defiance, but I don't have a chance to say anything before the door is kicked in and three men enter.

"Hakawati," the first man says. "We've come for you and that ill-borne girl of yours."

5

THE MEN GRAB ME, PULLING at my arms.

Layala's scream fills my head, and I spin around, kicking the man holding me.

"You let go of my child!" I yell and shove my way like a bull toward the man roughly handling her. He lets go, startled, and I push my body between him and Layl's.

"Get out of my house," I demand with as thunderous a voice as I can summon.

"Your girl threw animal shit at my boy," the first man says.

"Your boy bothered my girl in the marketplace," I reply. "She had every right."

"Your kind is long gone, jinn," the second man, the one who grabbed Layl, says. "We imprisoned your kind, *killed* your kind, and we can do the same with you." He pulls a necklace from under his tunic and dangles it before me. It's a small lamp, topped with a golden lid. "A jinn is stuck in here. This could be you, too. Only Sheikh Hamadi's word keeps us from slitting your throats."

"You're going to regret not raising that girl of yours to show more respect!" the third intruder snaps.

I spit in his face then. He wipes the dribble away with his sleeve and snarls at me. "You will pay for this, jinn. You and your child!" He points a finger at Layala, and I resist the urge to bite his finger off.

"Leave," I say, my voice a bit shaky. "And don't return. You're not welcome here."

"*You* won't be welcome here much longer," the third man says. "Not if we have any say in it."

"Without me, your land will be overrun with ghouls!" I say. "Without me, ghouls would snatch your children in the night, tear them limb by limb, and leave their bodies behind for the vultures. Is that what you want? Is it?" My voice is hoarse now, and one of the men's faces is drained of color.

"There are other hakawati jinn," the first man says. "You're not the only one. We could drag another from the ends of the earth and let them manage our dead souls here. And perhaps," he says, leaning closer to me, "perhaps these stories of ghouls are nothing but stories, stories *you've* woven to keep us from slipping into your home at night and ridding us of you."

I blanch at the thought, but keep my chin held high. "My bloodline has long been killed off. I'm the last one on this side of the ocean. And the ghouls are as real as the blood in your veins and the lungs in your chest."

"Then fulfill your role, Hakawati. There has been talk of a creature entering town. Stories are brewing that it could be a ghoul. Could be nothing but imagination, but if it is real, if ghouls are real, then do your job, Hakawati. Or we will find another who will."

The man holds my stare, then flicks his eyes over to Layala, who is just behind me.

I wave a wooden spoon in their faces, threatening to slap them with it. They laugh but they leave, and that is all I want.

Without thinking, I run outside, wooden spoon still in hand. "Never return here again!" I shriek. "If you do, I will turn you into clay, and I will smash you into pieces as fine as dust. And then I will scatter your dust to the wind."

The men stare at me, and one of them makes as if to grab me. But I slap him away with my spoon.

"Go!" I scream. "The sheikh will hear of this. You threatened his granddaughter; he will not take kindly to that."

They run off, and I turn back to my home, to Layala.

But when I step inside, she is not alone.

A woman stands before her, dressed in red, with a black sash tight around her slim waist. Her hair is long and wild, flowing down her back in twisting tendrils. She is bent over Layl, who's sitting in a chair, staring up at the woman with wide, dark eyes.

"Move away from my child," I say.

The woman turns around, a smile on her face. "Hakawati," she says, "it's been a while. I was just telling your daughter about—"

"Leave," I interrupt.

The woman shrugs and glances back to Layala. "You think about what I said, girl. And let me know—"

"Leave!" I yell, and the woman faces me once more.

"You should get that door fixed, you know," she says as she shoves past me. "Who knows what depraved soul could enter your home."

I watch her red back fade down the path away from our home before I confront Layl.

"What did she say?" I ask.

But Layala shakes her head. "I . . . let's fix the door, maman. It's cold."

The door hangs crookedly on its hinges, and the rain gusts in heavier now, water splashing into the house, seeping into the wood floor.

"Come, Layl," I say, knowing Layala is right. "Help me hang a curtain to keep the rain and wind out."

We take an old sheet and nail it above the doorway, blocking out some of the elements, but tonight, tonight we'll sleep cold and wet.

"I'm sorry, maman!" Layala cries. "It's my fault."

"No, hiyati, none of this is your fault." I wipe at her tears and move to spread some honey and cinnamon over a slice of bread.

"Eat this," I tell her. "A little sugar makes everything sweeter."

She smiles gratefully and bites off a piece, chewing it slowly.

I smile back at my child, but inside, my heart feels as heavy as a ship's anchor. I want to sink into the earth and not rise. But this is not a luxury I have; no mother does.

Instead, I grab a paper and a pen, writing a note to Sheikh Hamadi, Layala's grandfather.

"What are you writing?" she asks, looking over my shoulder.

She snatches at the sheet, crumbling it in her hand before flinging it into the fire. "No! I refuse to go live with jido. I won't leave you, not with men banging on the door in the dead of night."

"You must, kushtbani. It is safer at his house. He has stone walls and hired guards. He can keep you safe—"

"No." Her face screws up the same way it was when she was born, angry and defiant. "What about *you?* Who will keep *you* safe, maman?"

"Layl," I say, taking another sheet of paper. "It will only be for a short time, until those men have calmed down. Let the dust settle, and you can return. Besides, you love going to your jido's," I can't help but add, noticing the sudden flush in her cheeks.

"Layl, I don't know how long it will be, or how safe—"

"I don't care! You can't throw me aside at jido's and expect me to stay there! You'll come back and I'll be married off to some old man and already be carrying his child."

"Layl!"

"Maman!"

I sigh at the heavens and wish Illyas was here, a living man, a husband and a father. But he is not, and I'm the only parent around.

"Please, Layl," I say. I hear the exhaustion weighing down my voice. "It's only for a little while."

"I'll go for a few days only," she states, wiping her sticky hands on a cloth. "But then I come back home."

"You'll return when the dust has settled. Now stop arguing with me and go pack your things."

"You should come, too," she suddenly adds. "To jido's. He won't say no. And the seeds will fall wherever you are."

I wince at hearing another lie I told her when she was young. *Maman, when I grow up, can we go somewhere far away? Somewhere near water?*

Yes, hiyati, anywhere you want.

I didn't have the heart to tell her we were tied to this house, to this village—the outskirts of it—because of me.

And the seeds, they will come with us?

Anywhere I go, they will fall. Don't worry your head about it, hiyati.

The weight of all the small lies I told her over the years is burying me and, one day, it will crush me. It will be my fault.

"Come, Layala," I say when she's packed a meager bag of belongings. We dash out of the house into the pouring rain. Mud splatters up our legs, soaking through our boots.

"I miss the fire already," she whines, the wind almost snatching away her words.

"You'll have a greater fire at your jido's, with servants and a cook to make you the best meals."

"I prefer ours," she says simply. "They use too much oil in their food, and the meats are always swimming in it."

I can't help it; I laugh at the look on her face. She blinks at me in confusion, but I don't say anything as we race down the long path that meanders around the forest's edge behind our home. It leads right into town, up to the empty market stalls.

Horse hoofprints are etched in the mud-soaked road, lines following behind them from the wagon they must have pulled shortly after the rains began. The market is empty, save for loose curtains billowing in the wind and the area's single flickering gas lamp.

"I heard them say they wanted to put up another," Layala says, pointing at it. "After that woman was attacked last month."

33

"What woman?" I ask.

She bites her lip. "I thought you would have heard. I over-heard some girls talking about it the other day. It was that maid—the tax collector's—she said a ghoul or something like it attacked her. She had scratches down her arms and her face, and they said they found her bleeding in the road, shaking and mumbling about her soul being taken from her."

Ghouls stealing souls? But the gate between death and life is strong, closed even. No ghouls should be getting out.

"Where is she now?"

Layala shrugs. "They sent her off to a head doctor, or so I heard."

I think back to the moments after the men broke into our home, the moments I left Layala alone. "Tell me what that woman told you," I say.

Surprise lights Layl's face, streaked with rainwater. "Who is she, maman?"

"Someone I knew a long time ago. What did she say?"

"I didn't understand, really. She asked me if I had magic and what I could do. If I was like you. And if I wanted to be like you. But maman, I thought you said I have no magic—"

"You don't, Layl," I interrupt, "and she has no right speaking to you."

I want to say more, but when I look down the road, I see we've traveled further than I realized.

A white-stone house with windows the height of a grown man stands high in the center of town. Green and red vines cling to the walls, some spreading over the single main bal-cony at the front of the house.

"All I want is a fire," Layala says and hurries toward the windows, our conversation all but forgotten at the thought of warmth and dry clothes. We're at her grandfather's now, and every part of my body is telling me to turn and walk away. To snatch my child from the grips of the man inside, to make myself invisible from him.

Two guards recognize Layl and move to hurry her inside from the rain, but I step in beside my daughter and take her hand. "I'll walk you inside," I offer.

She smiles at me, and it's worth it, though it means my having to see her grandfather.

We step inside, rain slopping off our clothes, the servants huffing as they wipe at the mud we've tracked in on the tiled floors.

Layala's coat is taken from her to hang above a fire, but the servants pay me no mind. I remove my own coat and drape it over my arm, still dripping wet.

"The sheikh will see you," a manservant says to Layala as he approaches us.

I turn to follow, but the servant steps into my path. "The sheikh will see the missus only."

"Oh, get out of my way," I say, waving him off. "She is my daughter, not his."

I step around the man, who is too stunned to stop me. I follow Layala into her grandfather's study and shut the door behind me.

Sheikh Hamadi stares at us over his desk.

"Layaloon, my girl," he says, rising to his feet to hug my daughter. He ignores me as if I am a ghost unseen.

"Abu Illyas," I say, referring to his position as Illyas's father, "Layala will be staying with you a few days, if you please."

"My only grandchild can stay for as long as she wants," he answers, not even looking at me. I want to snap my fingers in his face, to force him to look me in the eye, but I twist them together instead and hide them behind my back.

"Three men came to the house," Layala blurts. "They broke down the door."

Abu Illyas's eyes snap to mine. "What is this?"

"They are the fathers of village boys who were bothering Layala a few days ago. She retaliated, and they came to . . . speak . . . to us."

"Speak to you by breaking down your door? This will not do." I know he is thinking of Layala's safety, not mine, but my heart melts—just a bit—at his love for my child. There is no love lost between us, I know, but he would give up his heart for Layl. "I'll have Abu Ishtar come to fix your door tomorrow," he says.

"*Shukran*," I say. *Thank you.*

He glances at me, eyeing my wet clothes. "You should have stayed in the foyer," he says. "Rather than bringing mud in here."

"And you should have kept your hands off of jinn magic instead of imprisoning jinns, but you never mention *that*."

Layala takes a sharp breath, her eyes flicking between her grandfather's face and mine, and I almost regret saying anything. Almost.

"Leave," Abu Illyas commands.

"I'll stay the night with my child and leave in the morning."

He says nothing except to call for a servant. "Have two rooms made up," he says.

"One is fine," I say. "We will share."

He doesn't reply, but speaks to the room as if I'm not in it. "The evening meal will be served in an hour. I suppose you'll invite yourself to that as well."

I say nothing as the servant ushers us away and up a staircase to a line of rooms.

"This one," she says, opening a door and letting us through. Layala enters it, as familiar with its layout as I am of the moles on her face and arms.

"Why did you tell jido that?" she asks. "What did you mean?"

I know what she's referring to. "Tonight, hiyati, I will tell you a story. But for now, let us go eat and warm our insides."

She pauses, then nods. "I *am* hungry," she says. "But after, tell me what you meant." Then she adds, "I've missed your stories."

36

And I realize, between telling the stories of the dead, I haven't told my own child a story in a long time.

Am I failing you, Layala? Am I failing you as your mother?

But I shake my head of the familiar thoughts and follow her out the room and down to the dining hall.

6

ABU ILLYAS SITS AT THE head of the long table, grabbing at his food with pieces of flatbread in between slurping his tea. The meats are layered with thick slices of tomato, simmering in herbs and, like Layala said, swimming in oil. The salad of parsley, onions, and lemon juice is ripe with pieces of dates and green olives.

The room is built of thick auburn wood, scenes of hunts and harvests carved into the paneling. The floor is made of tiles of layering colors, laid out in geometric patterns that would be dizzying if they were not so beautiful. A fire blazes in the fireplace just to the right of the room. Hanging above it, like the moon in the sky, is a rich oil painting of a young man, a beautiful woman, and a baby boy sitting on her lap. Abu Illyas, his wife, and Illyas as a baby.

The painting was commissioned by the most talented— and most expensive—painter in the land, a jinn. The colors he created were made from the clay he harvested and infused with his clay magic; he produced colors so rich, no one else, human or jinn, could reproduce them. During the jinn wars, when jinn tribes were already weak and many of the warriors slain, Abu Illyas had the jinn painter imprisoned in a metal box filled with the very paints he mixed.

Abu Illyas says little, except to tell Layala to take more food because "men like more meat on their women," and that she "should find a husband soon, as she is getting older."

I want to tear my child out of his house and away from his talk of women and men. Instead, I scrape at my food and chew hard to keep myself from talking.

"You weren't much older than Layaloon when you gave birth," Abu Illyas says, his voice cutting through the room. "It's time we start looking for a husband for her. Before she . . . gets herself into trouble," he says with a flash of his eyebrows.

"She's fourteen," I say.

"Older than you were when you started digging your claws into my only son."

Layala jerks her head between us, her tiny mouth open.

I hold back a retort for her sake, instead saying, "When she is older, she will choose her own husband. Until then, she is *my* child." I stare pointedly at him, and though his jaw clenches, he says nothing more.

The meal ends, and Layala and I are ushered out of the room, Abu Illyas complaining about the cold and ordering a servant to build the fire higher. We pad up the stairs and throw ourselves onto the large bed. It's wide enough that we can sleep on either side and still not touch.

"You promised me a story," she says, settling under the covers. She fluffs her pillow and turns on her side to face me.

I slip in beside her under the covers, but lay on my back, staring up at the ceiling. It's painted a rich blue, inlaid with golden stars and a moon so bright, it shines even in the dark. More jinn magic.

I take a deep breath and tell her my tale.

Jinns were beautiful creatures, powerful in the elements, caretakers of the dead. They had power humans did not have and wanted for themselves.

Humans came to jinns, befriending them, seducing them, manipulating them. Some became true lovers; others, true enemies. But the jinns didn't realize humans were enemies until it was too late.

One day, a young jinn girl fell in love with a young human boy. The boy was the son of a town elder, the only son. In fact, he was the only child. His mother had died in his youth, and his father never loved another woman after her. The boy grew up knowing no want, for his father gave his son everything his pockets could offer.

The two young lovers met in the town's souk, as the jinn's mother sold her stories in the market. The jinns were known for their skills, either weaving, or singing, or growing, or storytelling. They were a respected people, so much so that kings and queens came to them for their skills.

The young boy noticed the jinn girl, and he sought her out. First with a smile, then with a book of stories, and finally, he approached her to speak to her.

The parents did not know, and that was the lovers' first mistake. Their second mistake was in continuing the first until it was too late. Late enough to produce a child when they were children themselves and would lose the support of their families. But that came later.

They spent illicit nights together, the jinn telling the human of her peoples' secrets. The boy recorded her stories, not for ill use, but to remember them, for he was so in love with her he wanted to immortalize every one of her tales. He didn't want to forget a single word she told him.

But the boy was foolish, for he left his book of jinn secrets and stories out on his desk for his father to find. His father, though generous with his son, was a greedy man, who wanted all the riches the world could offer and more.

The father stole the book, and though the boy searched high and wide, he could not find it, for his father had taken it to the other town elders and they decided they would steal the jinn secrets.

But they found they could not get the jinns to do their bidding. For some jinns have a special power above all else:

41

they can grant wishes. Not always, not exact, but they do have that magic if they are happy and free.

The humans did not know that a jinn must be free to grant a wish. So, in their stupidity, they imprisoned the jinns in metal amulets, in lamps, in wooden boxes, even in pieces of fabric. All the jinns scattered in the world were imprisoned or killed if they did not submit.

The humans then demanded wishes, but the jinns— unhappy and imprisoned as they were—could not grant them. When the humans tried to free the jinns, they found they did not have the power to do so, and to this day, jinns are still imprisoned.

The jinn girl was spared, because the babe she carried in her womb was that of the boy's—his father's only son.

Layala stares at me with wide eyes. "Is that you, maman? The jinn girl in the story?"

I nod. "And the human boy is your father."

"So, is the elder . . . is it jido?"

I nod again, stroking her hair back from her face.

She rolls over on her back and stares up at the ceiling. "I never knew."

"I never told you."

She looks at me. "Why?"

"Some stories are best left untold until their time comes."

"Is being a hakawati, the dead's keeper, *your* imprisonment?"

I'm surprised at her astuteness. "Yes. I—" I clear my throat, for I am about to undo a lie I've told her. "My imprisonment is a bit different. Your father begged his to spare me because your bones were still in my body and not yet born. His father—Sheikh Hamadi—complied, but refused me complete freedom. He imprisoned me in the cottage and made me Hakawati, which was to be my bloodright passed down from my mother. But a jinn hakawati's role is to preserve her tribe's

42

stories and history, to tell the tales of her tribe's dead so they are not forgotten. My role now is to tell the tales of all dead, no matter their tribe. And that is a different type of life."

Layala's eyes close and, for a moment, I think she's fallen asleep. But then she flicks them open and looks me deep in the eyes the way she held my gaze as an infant.

"You're bound to the cottage?"

"Yes."

"You can't leave it? I thought you could."

"I can leave it, but I can't go far. Not without first breaking the magic."

"How would you break the magic?"

"I don't know, hiyati."

"Who would know?"

"Jinns," I say, before realizing my mistake. If she is spending time with a jinn boy, this will likely spur her to spend more time with him, if only to find out how to free me. "But they are all imprisoned," I add quickly. "The ones who matter."

"And the jinns who are free?"

"There aren't any free ones who are worth their salt. If a jinn seems free, they are likely slaves to another's will, and that will can never be pure and good."

Layala pauses, not looking at me. "So, you lied to me, about being able to live elsewhere."

It's not a question.

"Yes."

My daughter purses her lips, and I see a change on her face. She realizes that, because I have lied, she has a right to have her own lie. She doesn't feel guilty for her jinn boy, and that frightens me.

7

I STEAL INTO THE EARLY morning while the sky is still deciding what color it wants to be. Layala stirs and I kiss her before I leave. My heart aches, seeing her long limbs spread out on the bed; when did she grow so much? She used to fit into my side, curled up with her hands tucked under her chin. Now she's almost as tall as I am.

"I'll come get you once I think it's safe," I tell her.

She mumbles something sleepily, then turns to her side and falls back to sleep. I stare at her long, tangled hair fanned out on the pillow. It's a rich black, like my mother's. I pull the blanket up to her chin and tuck it in around her, as if a piece of fabric could keep her safe from the world.

I'm tempted to take her into my arms and carry her back home, to lay her in her own bed where she belongs. But I resist the urge. *She's safer here, with guards at the house and a wealthy grandfather to keep harm away.*

But if ghouls are attacking young girls, no guard, no amount of riches, can keep her safe.

I shake my head of the thoughts. *The servant* said *it was a ghoul. Who's to know she knew what she saw?*

So I slip on my cloak and steal out of the house. I tilt my head down against the wind, leaves crunching underfoot. For a moment, a man's voice floats on the air before being snatched away in the wind, but when I scan the trees on either side, I see no one.

The path is wide enough for one person, splitting off the side of a main road for horse carriages and the gypsy wagons that come through once a year to sell their wares and services in the souk. I remember the gypsies as a child. We jinns and the gypsies lived the life of tribal law and heritage, and we shared with each other our secrets and power. Now, the gypsies keep their heads low to keep them on their necks. They stay away from most towns unless traveling through or selling things. I don't blame them.

Again, I hear a man's voice. It sounds distant, but I can't tell because of the wind. I throw back the hood of my cloak, listening for any sounds.

I hear it again.

A low sound, moaning and . . . in pain?

It's coming from my left, off the path and into the woods.

"Hello?" I call out, then curse myself for my stupidity. What if it's a trick? A bandit preying on a lone traveler.

Or a ghoul. If one catches me, it will suck out my marrow and fry my fat for its meal, if it doesn't steal my body for its own.

I bundle myself tighter in my cloak and lift my hood back up around my head. The sun is rising now, and light is spreading out around me. It is morning, and the dead need me. I force my legs faster to my cottage, forgetting about men and ghouls.

The front of my house is littered with pomegranate seeds, but they look different. I bend down to grab a few, finding their edges browned, though their center is still red like a beating heart.

"Strange," I say to myself, and my face crinkles with worry. "I'll ask Illyas about this."

I go inside the cottage, stepping over the splinters of my door. The sheet Layl and I hung up is still there, soaking wet from the rain the night before. My floor is stained with water, and my weight sinks into the soft wood as I step over it.

I sigh, taking my jars off my shelf, and hurry to the cemetery.

Illyas meets me when I'm back in death.

"Hiyati," he says, "you look worried."

"Something strange has happened, but first, I have to tell you that Layala is with her grandfather."

"She decided to spend the night with him? Or was she with the jinn boy again?"

"I took her to her grandfather, and I'm keeping her there until I think it's safe."

Illyas's eyebrows furrow and his mouth dips into a frown.

"Those boys who were bothering her, their fathers came to our house. They broke our door, and—" My voice catches and Illyas moves as if he is going to hold me. But of course, his arms go through me. "Death, she came."

"Nado," he says, his play on my name. "Nadine. Tell me."

"I can't keep her safe. Not with men barging into my house, men I'm half the size of, who could take me over their shoulders and throw me down a well without thinking twice of it. I wish . . ." I start, but then shake my head.

"Wish what, hiyati?"

"I wish you were still alive. And that you were there with me, with us."

His face melts and I sense the guilt wringing his heart.

"I know you sacrificed yourself, Illyas, but sometimes I wish you didn't."

"I had to!" he says, his voice rising harsh against the silence of death. "I did what I needed to keep you both safe."

"I know, and I am grateful."

"But?"

"But it's hard. Still," I say, forcing my back straight. "I will manage. But I think something is wrong, wrong with death itself. The seeds, they were brown? I don't understand it."

Illyas's frown dips deeper. "And you said Death came somewhere? Was she at the house?"

I nod. "She came and spoke to Layala, but I don't know much of what she said. Layl told me Death asked her if she had magic—"

"What is she doing around Layala?" he interrupts.

"I don't know, Illyas. I really don't. And I am so frightened."

"You have to do something, Nado. You keep our girl safe and out of that woman's clutches."

"I will, you know this." I realize I'm gasping now, struggling for breath.

"Nado," he says. "I know you will keep our girl safe. And yourself, take care of yourself, too."

I nod, but I want to sob, to curl up in Illyas's arms and to be held, for once.

"Hiyati, try not to worry so much. Layl is a smart girl. She will make the right choices."

"Like throwing horse shit at boys in a marketplace?" I say with a choked laugh.

Illyas chuckles but then sobers. "Keep safe, hiyati. And fix the door as soon as you can."

"Your father said he will send someone to do it."

"Good, good," Illyas says, and his face darkens. "It's the least he can do for you."

He reaches over to give me a hover-kiss, and I soak in his warmth. For a moment, I think I can smell him, but I know that is just the ghost of a memory.

"Goodbye, Illyas," I say, and leave death.

I return to the cottage and fulfill my hakawati duties for the morning. There are fewer dead again today, but I try not to worry much about it.

Instead, I crush herbs and make a few brews with them, storing them in little glass bottles. When villagers get sick enough, they ask me for medicines, and my stores have been running low. Best be prepared for the winter when even the healthy fall ill.

Abu Illyas's man comes by later that day to fix the door. He arrives with two others, who carry a new wooden door atop a carriage. They say little to me as they work, only thanking me for the tea I offer them, then calling out goodbye when they leave, though I am sure one glares at me as he is leaving.

I settle in for the night, checking the new locks on my door twice before turning my back to it and toasting my cold feet by the fire. I almost call out to Layl to join me, then remember she's in another house, in another bed, keeping warm by another fire.

I awaken Saqr, and he shakes his sleepy head. "Make sure my girl is fine," I say. "And happy."

He flies out the window, and I leave it open a slit for when he returns.

Cool air swirls in through the window, and I shiver against it, moving back toward the warm fire and the tea brewing atop it.

8

THE MORNING BRINGS ME AN empty ground.

Not a single seed this morning, and that is more worrisome than anything else. There have always been the dead.

Things are no longer strange; they are wrong. And wrong means trouble.

I hurry back to the cemetery, spying a wolf lurking around. They don't come close to town or leave the woods much, except in winter when they are hungry and steal goats or chickens. It seems to saunter away, but still I keep an eye on it as I settle over a grave and press my palms to its dirt.

But no lightning strike comes.

"Illyas?" I say, filling another cup of dirt water and drinking it, ignoring the rich silt that chokes the back of my throat.

Instead of the usual silvery light of death, I see the mottled grey of the border between life and the Waiting Place of death. It's as if I'm underwater and sunlight is piercing through the water above my head.

But it feels odd here, not only because I never come here, but because my movement is slurred, like the time I drank too much *arak* when I found out I was pregnant and tried to do away with the child. I got drunk and vomited for two days after, but the child clung to my womb.

Of course, I'm grateful Layala was fierce, even in the womb.

"Illyas!"

He doesn't hear me or come to me, and I'm stuck sitting on top of a grave, a wolf just feet away from me.

I try again, thinking of Illyas's face, his smile, his warmth, even in death. But for the first time, death bars my entry into it.

This is worse than trouble; this is danger.

And so is the wolf.

9

THE WOLF STREAKS TOWARD ME in a ball of white and grey. I shriek, then catch myself, knowing panic will do me no good. I'm still hunched over the grave, but I roll to the side and the wolf swerves to avoid slamming into a gravestone.

"Stop," I tell the beast, and it freezes its attack. It stalks toward me, teeth bared, but it doesn't strike. It can't.

"Leave," I command.

The wolf growls, but its legs do my bidding. It turns, its muscles rippling against my command, fighting its own body, but it slinks off into the woods.

I let out my held breath and slump to the ground, my legs shaking as a newborn colt's. The little animal magic I have drains me quicker than even storytelling does. I'm surprised the magic worked; it rarely does unless I am frightened enough.

Just as my pulse is settling, the wolf returns.

I'm caught unawares as the animal darts through the air and crashes into my chest. I struggle to breathe, both against the force of its strike and the wolf's weight on me. Its breath is tangy and sour, its teeth yellowed. The eyes are grey and glint like slick blood under moonlight.

It snaps its jaws in my face, threatening but not yet biting, then blows hot air through his nostrils, right into my face.

"I gave you a chance," I warn, then press my thumb into the center of its forehead, just above its snout. The wolf falls over in a flash of pale ochre, and I'm left with the figure of a clay wolf. "You should have taken it."

I pocket the statuette and make my way home, deciding I will set the wolf on the shelf next to where I keep Saqr. Halfway home, a man's voice calls, the same one from earlier. I turn my head, believing it's coming from my right, from within the woods, but I can't be sure.

I slip my hand into my pocket, considering bringing the wolf to life. But I let it be. Cocking my ear, I strain to hear the voice. But the woods are silent now, the air still and empty. *I'm losing my mind.*

But I know better than to believe that. Once I'm home, I lock the door and block it with my table, hoping the weight will hold back an intruder. I shut the window I'd kept open a slit for Saqr—just in case. When dark falls, I slip into bed and for the first time in years, sleep with a knife under my pillow.

I'm awoken a few hours later by a knock at the door. It is still dark enough that I have to light a candle as I stumble into my slippers. My skin is raised with cold from the night—and from the feeling that something isn't right. Something more than a stranger knocking in the dead of night at my door. I clutch the knife's handle so hard, it digs into my skin.

I grab the clay wolf from where I set it on the shelf beside Saqr and slip it into my nightrobe's pocket. If I need protection, I'll awaken the wolf and send it attacking.

The person—*I hope it's a person*—knocks again, more insistent this time. The new door has an eyepiece, and I spy through it, leaning over the table as I do so.

There's a man on the other side, his face layered with a thick beard, leaves and twigs stuck in it. I blow out my candle and check that the curtains are drawn. They're thick enough that he won't be able to see through them.

He knocks again, harder, as if he's rapping with the head of a cane. But he's not, because I can still see him through the eyepiece. His hand looks meaty, thick with flesh and bone.

His face is wide, eyes slanted like a wolf's. I feel my body tense and my heart stuttering, just as it did when the wolf attacked me. I don't like the look of this man.

Instead of opening the door, I ease away from it, sliding off my slippers so I can pad silently in the dark.

I hear the man stalking around the house, no doubt angling for a way in. But everything is locked, and the window is secure with its thick glass and lock. I peek around the curtain. He's keeping a distance from the house now, as if repelled by it. Maybe he doesn't like the thorn bushes Layala planted along the cottage's rim to keep animals—and other creatures—away.

He circles once, then twice, before he returns to the door. He tries the lock, but it's solid metal. I send up a blessing for Abu Illyas, much different than my usual curse; he at least sent a solid door to replace our broken one.

Perhaps the men from earlier were a blessing in disguise; because of them, I got a new door, much sturdier than the old one.

The man huffs, and I slink back to the door's eyepiece. I nearly scream when I spot an eye right up to it. But he can't see in, and I bite the tip of my tongue to keep quiet.

I want to shout at him to leave, that there is nothing here worth stealing. But it's best not to let him know a woman is in here, alone. I thank heavens I had the wisdom to send Layala to her grandfather, that she is safe behind stone walls and thick doors.

He tries the lock once more before he turns around and leaves, favoring one leg, the other caked in dried blood. For a minute, I think of opening the door; he may only want medicine.

He stumbles down the front pathway, and I hear him grunt, even through the door. I see something dark puddle under him: blood.

He's only an injured man in need of medicine and some wound cleaning. Not a thief, not a murderer.

I chew on my lip for a moment, then heave the table away. I fling open the door and dash out into the chill of the night.

"Are you injured?" I ask.

The man spins around, grunting. "Yes, you the healer?"

"I have medicines, mostly herbs. I can give you what you need."

"I don't have much money," he says, but hobbles toward me, a gleam in his eyes.

I step back and check that I still have the wolf and knife in my pocket. The wolf is there, but the knife is not. My gut clenches when I realize I set it on the table when I slid it out of the way and I curse myself for being stupid.

"Come in," I said. "I have little, but you're welcome to it."

"Shukran," he says.

He follows me up the path, and I try to keep an eye on him in my periphery. He's shuffling, his gait off with the injured leg, but his arms and shoulders look strong, sturdy, and more than capable of throwing me across my kitchen. He carries a pack slung over one shoulder, bulging with items that clink inside.

"Watch your foot," I say, pointing to the step that leads up into the house.

He grunts and grabs his injured leg to swing it into the house. "Damn wolf got me," he says. "Big grey one."

I smile and finger the clay wolf in my pocket. "I'm sure it won't bother you again, mister—"

"Just call me by my name; no need for mister. It's Wissam."

"Nadine," I say. "Shut the door behind you," I add. "And have a seat. Do you want tea?"

"Something stronger if you have it," he says with a dry laugh, grimacing as he eases himself into a chair and scrapes it closer to the fire. He grabs a small log and throws it into the hearth, stoking the flames until they're blood red and hot.

I smell him now, musty as a grave, like wet earth and stone. *Must be sweat from traveling.*

"I don't, sorry," I say. "But I have black mushroom tea. Strong and earthy."

The man grunts and I take it to mean it'll suit him well enough.

"What happened?" I begin, boiling water for both the tea and to clean the man's wounds.

"It came out of nowhere. This blur of grey and it just attacks. Nearly bit off a chunk of my leg, but I managed to kick it off and run. It got away before I could shoot it down with arrows. I hope it doesn't go into town to terrorize the chickens."

I laugh, and I'm surprised to hear myself. Color blooms across his cheeks, but there's a glint in his eyes that matches the fire.

I cut up a few pieces of cloth and boil them in the water.

"I'm sure it disappeared somewhere and won't be bothering anyone," I say, turning around, holding out a spoon with steaming cloths hanging from it.

But instead of an injured man sitting in a chair, I find a ghoul standing before me, a devilish grin on his face.

"*Marhaba*, jinn," he slurs. *Hello.* "I believe you have something of mine."

10

HE STRETCHES A LEATHERY HAND out to me, palm facing up. His face is wrinkled and lined with welts.

His skin is tan, like wet soil, and two short horns stab out from either side above his mouth.

I fling the steaming cloths in his face and dash around him, snatching the knife off the table. I'm by the door, but he shoots forward, faster than a breath, and blocks my way.

"Not so fast, jinn," the ghoul says. All trace of his human facade has vanished, and his face is covered in thickened skin, the teeth long and rectangular.

"Leave, ghoul," I say. "Only the living belong here. Your place is a cemetery; go, there is one behind the house, and there is a stream there, the one fed from death itself. Go there."

"Not without my wolf, jinn," he argues, stretching his hand out to me again. "I watched you turn my beloved into clay; I want it back, in flesh and blood."

"I threw it into the fire," I lie, hoping he will leave if he believes his wolf isn't around anymore. *Or he will be angry and kill you for it.* "Now go, leave!"

The ghoul eyes me, then shoots his hand out, catching my neck.

His grasp tightens until I am gasping for breath and pounding at his arm with my fists. He doesn't let go, and I know he will squeeze the life out of me and not feel a touch of remorse. I choke, struggling for breath as I slice the knife at his arm layered with skin as thick as bark.

Then I do what Illyas once taught me: pinch the soft flesh between the thumb and forefinger and keep pinching until the attacker lets go.

It seems the ghoul is no different than a human and, in a few breaths, he howls in pain and his hand shoots away from my neck.

"Jinn!" he spits through clenched teeth, as if cursing my kind.

"Here, take it," I say, flinging the clay wolf at him. I swing open the door and step aside. "Now leave."

"I said, in flesh and blood. You have given me clay earth instead. Bring my wolf back to life."

I eye the ghoul, then dart my chin in the direction of the table. "Set it there and step outside. I will bring it to life, but then you must leave."

"Yes, yes," he says, his eyes blazing. He moves to set the statuette on the table, but he doesn't budge from it.

"Outside," I repeat, "or I'll take the wolf and shatter him into a thousand pieces."

Fear, then anger, flashes across the ghoul's face.

"I can kill you like that," he says with a snap of his fingers. "Then what will happen to your precious daughter, Hakawati?"

He knows about Layala? "Touch a hair on my child's head, and I will make sure you find yourself in Jahannam."

The ghoul rears back its head and laughs. "Pretty words from a jinn. But hurry up and bring the wolf back. I'll be on my way once you do."

I grab the wolf and dash outside. Just as I expect, the ghoul follows, eyeing the statuette in my hand. I circle around him until my back is to the house and his back is to the woods beyond. My hands hover over the wolf, my magic commanding it to life.

It grows warm under my touch, clay becoming skin becoming fur. And before it grows to full size, I fling it at the ghoul and dash back into the house. I slam my door with enough force that it rattles the window, and I slide the table against the door.

Looking through the eyepiece, I know both ghoul and wolf are gone now.

But ghouls have long memories, and they don't take kindly to jinns. This one will be back, and he may not come alone.

11

MORNING DOESN'T COME FAST ENOUGH, and I am up and boiling tea before the sun's light streaks into my cottage.

I haven't slept since the ghoul's visit, and I doubt I will sleep tonight—or the night after—no matter how tired I'll be. My gaze keeps flitting to the window, half-expecting to find a wolf pacing the front of my home. The thought occurs to me to tell Layala to add a few more of the poison leaves she planted behind the house, then I remember she's not here. My heart aches with missing her.

But she's better off with her grandfather. She's safer there. If she were here when the ghoul was . . . I chase the thought away. *She wasn't, and that's all that matters.*

Layala is a human girl, she has no magic, she is safe, she is fine, she is healthy.

I repeat that to myself like the old shamans used to chant their prayers.

She is safe, she is fine, she is healthy.
She has no magic, she is safe, she is fine, she is healthy . . .
She is safe . . .

As soon as the sun is strong outside, I open my door and step out. No seeds litter my doorstep, and my blood runs cold. Two days without the dead is impossible. If there's one constant in life, it is the dead and the dying.

Leaves rustle above my head and, when a wind drafts through, they fall at my feet like clumps of brushed hair. I can't help but wish the fallen leaves were soul seeds, and my fingers twitch, eager to pick them up.

But then I spot an unwelcome face coming up the path to my home, the face of a young jinn.

What is he *doing here? I don't have time for him.*

"Looking for something?" I ask. He's steps away but hasn't noticed me standing in the middle of the path, blocking the curve to my home.

He startles and glances up, hand to his chest. It's most certainly Layl's jinn boy—same dark gray eyes and pale skin, with hair tipped in flames. He smiles, but I can tell it's forced.

"Yes. You."

He smiles wider, his teeth silvery and gleaming.

"I see," I say. "For what reason?"

He flicks his gaze behind me, at the cottage. "Mind if we go inside? The wind is picking up."

I sniff once, then nod, and turn toward the cottage. He follows me and shuts the door behind. I notice he doesn't lock it and a bit of the tension in my shoulders eases.

"*Shay?*" I ask. "Or *ahweh?*" *Tea or coffee.*

"Tea is fine, shukran."

As I start a fire and set a kettle of water above it to boil, I glance at him.

"A dirty home is an unhappy home," he says, looking around my home. "But a spotless house is a soulless one."

"Abu Abaddi ibn Farazi," I say, referring to a poet long-dead.

"Wise man," the jinn boy says as I hand him a cup of tea and take a seat at the table.

"You said you were looking for me. What for?"

"I know Layala is your daughter. She is a smart girl," he starts. "And I have not encouraged her any more than a normal boy would."

Normal boy. You're a jinn, you can't fool me. "You let her stay over, did you not?"

He lowers his gaze for a moment, staring into his own cup of tea. "She likes to tell stories, you know. She likes to write them down and share them with me."

"You haven't answered my question."

He sighs and leans back. "I only wanted to tell you that I have nothing but good intentions toward Layala. I needed a friend, and she showed up, as if sent down from the heavens." He sips his tea, eyeing me over the rim of the cup.

I don't say anything.

"You're Hakawati," he says, breaking the silence as he throws his chin in the direction of my face. There's a birthmark above my eyebrow, a swirled spot that extends down the side of my face and crosses over my jaw to end at the corner of my mouth. All Hakawati jinn have this birthmark, with one showing up every generation.

"Yes," I say. "What are you doing here? Why haven't I met you before now? A free jinn is a rarity in these parts."

A muscle twitches at his jaw, but he doesn't deny my accusation. "I keep my head down and don't speak much. Layala only noticed me for what I am when I was ill and at the souk looking for some medicine. She told me her mother was a healer, but I didn't want to leave with her. I was feeling too weak and just wanted to get home. She walked me there and that's how we became friends."

"That doesn't answer how no one else has noticed a jinn among them."

His throat bobs a few times before he answers. "I'm careful," he tells me with a jut of his chin. "And, as I said, I keep my head down."

"And your family? Where are they?"

"My tribe escaped to live off the forest during the jinn wars, and then during jinn imprisonments after that. Not everyone escaped; well, most didn't really, but enough did that our bloodline continued."

The jinn wars. Jinn tribe against human tribe, with even the gyp-sies taking one side or another. Hundreds of jinns massacred, all because humans wanted to call jinns theirs.

"Good," I say, "we need more jinns in the world."

The boy smiles, nodding. "I couldn't agree more. Though, mine are in a bit of a predicament. One I wanted your help with."

"So, now we get to the truth," I say. "Of what you are doing here and why you really befriended my Layala."

He takes a sip of his tea, and his smile fades. "My fam-ily were imprisoned in clay figurines. I know Hakawati jinn sometimes have clay magic. I . . . Layala mentioned you have a clay bird? You bring it to life sometimes?"

"I do," I say. "But my clay magic is weak. Limited to turn-ing things into clay and bringing clay figures back to life."

"But surely," he continues, "you can resurrect the dead, so to speak. I have tried, and I *have* been able to resurrect bodies, but not clay."

"You've resurrected people?" I snap. "How?"

The young jinn shrugs. "I have death magic, or a touch of it, at least. But you, you must have it stronger—"

I'm waving a hand to cut him off before he's done talking. "My skills are limited only to sending the dead to a final rest or raising flesh and bone bodies. I'm sorry." My voice is firm, and for a breath, I think he will set his cup down and leave me be.

His face drops as he stands up from his chair, shaking his head. "There must be *something* you can do, something you can think of." His voice rises, and he paces the room.

"I'm sorry," I repeat. "My own family was imprisoned before my maman could teach me much. And you know how the imprisoned are—they lose their strength, too weak to string three words together, let alone teach magic."

"They're all I have left," the jinn says, his voice pleading. "Please. I just want my family resurrected."

I try to soften my voice as much as I can. "I wish I could help." I glance over him. "What kind of jinn are you?"

"I'm part shadow jinn."

So, he can slip into shadows cast by other things and blend in, with no one the wiser.

"That explains how you can pass through town without being noticed."

A small smile flits across on his face. "Humans never see what they don't expect."

Silence lingers between us for a moment.

"What do you *really* want with my Layala? Besides getting to me?"

"I . . . Well, like I said, I was searching for medicine. I heard there was a jinn living near the woods, and the other day, I stumbled across Layala in town. I needed medicine and she said her mother—you—are a healer of sorts."

"And you just *happened* to stumble into *my* daughter on your search?" I press.

"I-I asked around and heard about Layala being of jinn blood, so I thought—"

"I'd like you to keep away from her," I say, sharper than I mean to. "She's young, and it's not safe for her, being my daughter. If she's seen in your company, the company of another jinn, it will become even less safe for her."

"I wouldn't let harm come to her," he begins.

"Neither would I. So, I'll say it again: keep away from Layala. I don't want anyone seeing you two together and then targeting my child. Or you, for that matter."

The jinn licks his lips, then bows his head. "As you wish, Hakawati."

I nod once and hold his gaze for a moment. "What is your name?"

"Rami," he says. "My name is Rami."

"Shukran, Rami, for understanding. If you ever are in need of herbs again, come to me. I'll help you."

He dips his head once more, then moves to the door. I follow after him.

"One favor," he says as he steps across the threshold back outside. "Consider what I've asked you. Maybe you can think of something that will help me raise my family."

I pause, then say, "I will see what I can do, on one condition."

"Ah," Rami says. "Favor for a favor."

"I will ask my maman if she knows of a way to help you. If she does, I will do my best. If she does not, then you will have to accept that. But, if I ask my maman, then you must stay away from Layala and make sure she stays away from you."

A smile flashes over his young face. "Yes, *shukran, shukran,*" he says, taking my hand and kissing it. "*Shukran kteer.*" *Thank you very much.*

"Come back inside and shut the door," I say, "and draw those curtains."

I'm already pulling out a wooden chest tucked into the back corner of my cottage, hidden under layers of blankets. The chest is old, older than my mother, and its hinges creak as I lift up the lid. Inside is a single golden vase, stoppered with a piece of dried resin.

"Oh, maman," I sigh, shaking the vase and releasing the stopper.

Smoke unfurls, a mix of gray and white, lavender and olive. The colors shift until they come together into a solid shape. Maman stands before me, her skin and hair much paler than I remember, the color washed away like stones rubbed smooth by a river.

"Maman," I say, wanting to touch her, though my hand will go through her just like with Illyas. She is neither dead nor alive, not in life nor in death. But she *can* speak to me.

"Hakawati," my maman says, reaching out a hand to cup my face. Her hand hovers right near my skin, warm enough I can almost feel it against me. "Hiyati."

"Maman, I need your help."

My mother glances around my cottage. "Where is Layala?" Her eyes land on Rami. "And who is that?"

"At her grandfather's. But that is not why I called you out. This is Rami, a jinn."

Her eyes search mine. "What is it, hiyati?" Already, her colors are fading, her body dissipating into smoke that's eager to slip back into its vase.

"Clay figurines," I blurt out. "Can a hakawati bring them back to life?"

"Nadine," maman says, "you know you can, you know this. You have Saqr—"

"Not like Saqr, maman. I mean, jinns imprisoned in clay. Can I resurrect them?"

"Hm," she muses, "very little can help an imprisoned jinn, Hakawati. Even another jinn."

"There's nothing I can do? Not even a normal resurrection?"

I study Rami, who looks as if he is swallowing every word my maman says.

My mother is shaking her head, even as her body is dissolving back into smoke. She's almost faded away completely now. She opens her mouth to say something else, but the vase swallows her back and all is still again. With a sigh, I stopper the vase and settle it back into its chest, locking it shut and settling the pile of blankets over it. It will be some time before I can speak to her again. She's the weakest of all my family imprisoned, ill as she was when she was caught.

I turn to Rami. "I am sorry," I say. "There is nothing I can do."

Rami doesn't speak, only sits with his head bowed.

"Very well," he says finally, getting to his feet. "Shukran for your help, and I will do as I promised. I will keep away from Layala."

He leaves my home and hurries down the path. With each step he takes away from me, I feel more worried that, somehow, this young jinn boy will be my undoing.

But there's another being far more dangerous, bolder, darker, than any jinn boy. And she's the one I must now speak to.

12

THE RIVER IS SILVERY AND far colder than any mountain river should be. But fed from the waters of death itself, the river is the closest connection I have to the realm if I'm not able to go into death.

It burbles around the town, snaking in its shimmering silver and gold in the morning light. And the water is crisp and so cold, a headache shoots up when I stoop to drink from it. The humans think it's another river that flows from the mountain, the glacial top making the water run ice cold. None know it's a river that flows from death. It's a jinn secret, one we've kept hidden from the humans, especially during the jinn wars.

"Kamuna!" I call out, slipping off my clothes and shoes. My body is bare, and my skin rises in pinpricks against the cold. I watch as the water ripples across moss-covered stones, and I take care not to slip on them as I slide into the river. The water clutches at my ankles, my knees, my thighs, my bare breasts, rising up to close in around my throat. I gasp against the frigid shock, forcing myself deeper into the water.

"Kamuna! I am here!" I yell as I slip my head under the water.

I clutch at thin blades of grass growing in the river bed, pushing them out of my way.

My breath hitches in my chest, and I struggle against the need, the urge, to surface for breath.

Kamuna, where are you? Come to me.

But Death does no one's bidding but her own.

My chest feels about to burst, and I panic, my body screaming for air. I break the river's surface and choke as cold air hits my face. I greedily gulp in air, even as my teeth chatter.

"No need for all these dramatics," a husky voice says.

I gasp and spin around in the direction the voice came from.

"Kamuna," I say, rising from the stream. The water sluices down my breasts and hips, and Kamuna eyes me coolly.

"Clothe yourself, jinn," she says and offers me my clothes. "I will meet you at that hut of yours. I expect a hot cup of tea."

She leaves me on the river bank, clutching at my clothes and shivering as the wind blows over my bare, wet skin.

I hobble, running after her, trying to slip on my dress and shoes as I go.

Once again, I bask in the wisdom of sending Layala to her jido's. *She is safe, she is safe, she is safe.* And that is more than enough for me.

But right now, I have Death herself in my home, and I want nothing more than to purify my life of her.

I'm panting as I dash past my door and into my home.

A shadow forms in front of me, gathering light from around it until it becomes hair and flesh. It's a woman, just a hairbreadth shorter than me, with eyes like the sky and hair the color of fashioned clay.

Her body shifts more, taking on substance. Her skin settles into a deeper olive color, rich with golds and browns. Her hair melds into a bronze, streaked with strands of copper.

Death's lips are pulled down in a frown. Her brows, dark and thick as a finger, are slanted above her eyes, though I realize it's their natural angle and not an expression of anger.

"Hakawati," she greets with a smile I can't read. She turns to sit by the fire, draping one long leg over the other. "Where's that tea?"

I glare at her. "As if you don't know where the kettle is."

She smirks and shrugs, turning her gaze to the fire.

"At least you worked the flames," I say, "since you let yourself into my home."

Kamuna is dressed in the color of clotted blood, and on her feet are shoes made of shattered mirrors. She smiles, her lips as bright as a fresh wound. "Extra mint and honey, don't forget," she says, gesturing at the two cups of tea I now hold.

"I haven't forgotten, Kamuna," I say. "Not in death or in life."

She settles closer to the fire. "Pour me, Hakawati." I pour the caramel-colored tea for her.

"Honey," she says, and I offer her the honey I bought from the market lady.

Kamuna stirs in the honey, takes a sip of the tea to taste it, then pours in more honey before she settles back into the chair. "Nothing like the drabness of death to dull your senses, even in life," she says.

She turns her gaze to me. "Ha-ka-wa-ti." She enunciates each syllable, drawing it out, as if tasting each letter. A honey-eyed H, tangy A, sweet W, sour T. "You owe me a favor."

My tongue knows my answer before my mind does, and I'm talking before I'm thinking.

"Yes," I say.

I sit down, warming myself by the fire after such a cold swim. My fingernails are still blue, but some color is returning to them.

"Tell me, Hakawati, why have you been entering my realm so often lately?"

"No," I say. "*I* called upon you. And I want to know what you said to my child."

Kamuna shrugs. "She didn't tell you herself?"

"She doesn't understand enough to tell me. What do you want with my child, Death?" I demand, bristling with annoyance. And fear.

She sucks on her teeth, as if thinking, but she already knows what she wants and is only making a show of thinking about it. "I want to talk to your daughter, Hakawati."

My breath catches in my throat. "Why?"

Kamuna's gaze bores into me. "You asked, I answered. I only want to meet her, talk with her a bit."

"About what? Talk with my daughter about what?"

She holds up a hand, twisting it in the air. "She is touched by death, no? Raised from the dead as a child. I only want to know her better."

I force myself to remain seated in my chair, rather than bolting out the door and going straight to check up on Layala.

"She's death-touched," Kamuna repeats. "She will have my magic in her."

"What is it you *want?*" I snap, my blood as cold as the river. I remember just how much Kamuna can speak in riddles, and it annoys me.

"Your daughter, she isn't here?" Kamuna asks, again not answering my question. "Is she with Sheikh Hamadi, your father-in-law?"

"He is my daughter's grandfather," I say, "but not my father-in-law."

Kamuna's lips purse. "Ah, yes, that's right. Shame and dishonor, was it not, you falling with child by the sheikh's son and not a marriage ring or necklace to call your own."

My face no longer heats up when someone mentions my past in that light. "Youth and foolishness share the same bed," I say. "There's nothing to be done for it."

"Your words are true, Hakawati, but no matter the age, there is no excuse for foolishness. Still, we all make our own mistakes and pay the cost one way or another."

Her eyes narrow as she says, "Call your daughter home."

"With what? A pigeon? No."

"Last I remember, you have clay magic, no? Call that clay bird of yours and bring the girl home. I want to speak to her."

"Her name is Layala, and she is not home," I say evenly.

"A shame," Kamuna says. "I so wanted to have a few words with her."

"Tell them to me and I'll pass them on to her."

Kamuna throws her head back and laughs. "I know you, Hakawati, and not one of my words will be spoken in her ears."

"Tell me what you want with my child."

"The death magic in her—"

"No. She has none."

A keen glint sparks in her eyes. "Ah, that's not what I sense, Hakawati. Every soul resurrected, every person raised from the dead, I have a connection to them. And your Layala, she is death-touched. She has a piece of my soul in her, a piece of the fabric of death itself. When you raised her, you told a piece of my own soul story and gave it to her. She is as much me as she is you and her father."

I ignore those last words. Refuse to let them seep under my skin. "If you want to call in your favor, then call it of me, not Layala. I will help you."

Kamuna's lips pinch together. "You're not the one with the death magic, Hakawati, not the kind I need. But your daughter is."

I don't say anything about Layala. Instead, I turn to other worries. "For two days now, the dead haven't rained on my doorstep. Before that, their seeds were limned in brown. I want to know why."

Death sets her cup down and stares at me. Then she rises and turns to my cupboards, pulling out a jar of finely ground coffee. As she boils a pot of water and stirs in the finely ground coffee, she says, "My tree is ill. The leaves are browning and falling. Death is sick."

"The tree of life?" I ask, my hands shaking. "But that means—"

"Yes," she confirms, "something's happened to my soul seed."

"And I can't enter death as easily anymore."

She stirs cubes of rose-sugar into her black coffee now. After a few minutes of silence, she offers me a cup and sets her own on the table before her. I sip the drink at first, then gulp it back. Dark coffee grounds sit on the bottom of my cup, and I long to hear my mother's voice reading the images and telling me what my future holds.

Mmm, I remember her saying, holding my cup this way and that, as if angling for better light. *Mmm. I see . . . a long life. Filled with hardship, yes, but joy. The joy runs deep, deeper than the pain, though the pain is heavy.*

She looks up with her eyes as wide and sharp as a caracal's.

Your grounds are dark and thick, and they set upon each other heavily. You will suffer, girl, and you will suffer much. But you will know love, and you will know it strong.

Kamuna throws the last dregs of tea into the fire before setting her cup back down.

"Layala is the key to all your . . . troubles," she says, holding my gaze. "I said I only wanted to speak to her. Is that too much to ask? Like how we spoke now, two women conversing over cups of ahweh. It's rare someone touched by death lives for as long as she does with no health issues. You know this, Hakawati."

I eye her sharply. "Stay away from my child, Kamuna."

"You'll never find out what's wrong with death, Hakawati, not without me."

"The living and the dead will both suffer if I can't do my job. The dead will overrun death and will enter life and kill the living. Spare us all the pain and tell me what's wrong."

"I rarely do something for nothing. I've learned not to offer my services for free. You know this, as well," she adds.

"Your payment will be that the dead do not wreak havoc on the living, including yourself! For, if a hungry soul finds you, it will steal your skin and wear it as its own, until that skin rots and that soul goes looking for another!"

Kamuna says nothing, only purses her lips and eyes me darkly. "Well said. But this is *your* responsibility, and *you* must do whatever is necessary to set things right. I have no obligation to keep the living safe from the dead. *You* do, as Hakawati."

My breath comes in ragged gasps, and I will it to calm. "If—*if*—I let you see Layala, what will you speak to her about?"

"I only want to know how she feels, if she's experienced anything unusual."

"Unusual how?" I ask. "She is normal, healthy, and she is human. No magic."

"Oh, Hakawati, you and I both know the most powerful don't always show their magic young, and if they do, it's weak and petty. Some are, as we call them, *late bloomers*. Perhaps Layala, with her plant magic, has been showing signs of being death-touched, signs you've been ignoring—"

"She is human," I interrupt. "And will live a long, normal, happy life. Untouched by magic. She is no jinn."

"Your will may not be fate's will," Death says. "One hour," she says, holding up a finger. "One hour with her, and you get what you've asked for: to know what is making death ill and how to fix it."

I almost want to tell her to fix it herself, that death is *her* realm, and *she* should heal it, not me. But I know my job as Hakawati is important, and Death will keep her realm sick until she gets what she wants. But my duty is both to the living and the dead. And to Layala, above all else. If the dead overrun life, she would be in danger.

Kamuna should control her realm, not be controlled by it.

But then I hear the memory of my mother's voice. *Jinn and Death have always been both at odds and in arms together. The utmost duty of a Hakawati jinn is the protection of life and death, even if death cannot do the same. Remember the will of a jinn must be stronger than the will of others, Nadine, and let that be your guiding hand.*

"I want to get to know her, Hakawati. Is that a sin?" Kamuna says, interrupting my memories. "I am dying; you've seen the evidence. My seed is rotting, and nothing will hold back the rot unless I put it in holding waters. Even that won't work for all of time."

I'm shaking my head at Death, but she ignores me.

"I need someone to take over my position as Death. I am ready to pass on to Mote and be with my child. I can't do that unless I choose a replacement, and only those who have been death-touched and lived can do so. Layala was raised from the dead and has lived years after. She can—"

"My child will *not* take your place as Death! Absolutely not!" I hear myself spluttering. Spittle flies from my mouth, but I don't care. All I can think, *feel* is the hammering in my chest and the blood throbbing up to my head. *I must keep Layl safe. Above all else, Layala must be safe. But I cannot keep her safe if life is glutted with ghouls who cannot pass on to Mote.*

"Hakawati, listen to reason."

"No! You stay away from my child." I jab a finger in her direction, but it is quivering, and I know she notices.

"Her time is coming to an end, Hakawati," Death says. "You know this. You must know this. No one who has been raised, who is death-touched, lives a long life. But if you step aside and allow her to be Death, she will outlive even you."

"She will be *Death*. She will live in death. She will not be alive."

"Would you rather her be dead in a grave or alive in her own right, even if she lives in death itself?"

"Layala has years to live, and live them she will."

Kamuna's face melts into a frown and a sad look slips into her eyes. "The dead are dead, Hakawati. Look at me." She glances down at herself. "I am flesh and spirit in one, bone and teeth. I am *alive.*"

"But you are *dead.*"

"I am alive, Hakawati, in my own way. Layala would be, too."

My heart hammers, my blood sluggish, and I'm sure I'm going to faint. "It took you a generation, more, to be able to leave death at will and to remain outside it. Layala would not be able to return to life for years."

"She would still have a life. Death is more, more alive, more *everything*, than you've seen, Hakawati. It is more vast than you think. She would have a life."

"She would have no love, no home, nothing to keep her happy."

"She would."

"She would not, Death." I pause, then ask, though I'm sure I already know the answer. "Are *you* happy?"

"Facts aren't a threat, Hakawati, not unless you treat them that way. And the fact is, Layala would have been dead years now if it weren't for me. She should have stayed dead all those years ago. You bought her time, yes, but bought time runs out."

I notice she doesn't tell me whether she's happy.

"I don't want my child to die," I moan and my body gives out. I'm sprawled on the floor, my head hanging down, neck too weak to support it. I want to rip my heart out and throw it in the fire, just so I don't feel. "I can't let her die."

Kamuna kneels beside me, resting a hand on my shoulder. I shrug it off. "You can stop this. You can spare my child's life."

But she's shaking her head before I'm done speaking. "I am offering you both a way out," she says in a soft tone, as if trying to soothe a distraught child. "Let me speak to her, Hakawati. One hour, to see where her mind is. If I do not think she is a good fit, if I do not think she will be able to take my place, I will not force the situation."

She pauses. "Borrowed time must always be returned."

I think for one breath, then two, three, until ten breaths have passed. Then I speak.

"Tomorrow, I will bring Layala home for a single hour and not a moment more. But—" I say sharply, holding up my forefinger, "—I will be with her, and not for a breath will I be leaving her side. You will tell her nothing about being death-touched, nothing about magic, and do not, for even one second, make her feel she could be anything but a human girl."

Kamuna spreads her arms out and shrugs. "As you wish, Hakawati."

She eyes me as she says this, but something in her gaze falters. As if she is not quite telling me the full story. As if she is hiding something from me. And nothing frightens me more than Death herself lying to my face.

"I'll be back for your child, Hakawati," she says. "Layala, tomorrow, or I *will* force the situation. Your favor owed is hers, too."

"You will kill her in cold blood," I say, not ask.

"I will take back what I've given," Kamuna amends, "but it's the same to me."

"She will be here." With that, I turn my back on Death.

She turns to leave, stopping only for a breath at the door. "I heard you met that wretched jinn, Rami."

"What of him?" I ask, not surprised she's been keeping an eye on me.

"He should be kept from daughters. He killed mine."

"I have told him to stay away from Layala." But I know how weak my words sound.

"I wouldn't trust him, Hakawati. Not with the skin of my tooth or the marrow of my bones."

Death leaves the door open behind her, and a cold gust of air ruffles my hair and dress. I don't bother following after her; if she doesn't want to talk, then she will not talk.

The room feels too still and silent. I gather up the used cups, rattling them only for the noise as I settle them in a basin for washing later.

I drop to my chair, my bones feeling tired and old. But my heart is beating strong and fast, and all I can think is, *Death wants my baby.*

13

Tomorrow arrives and finds Layala sick in bed with a fever. Abu Illyas insists on calling for the town healer, but I wave him off.

"I'm a healer too, you know. My job isn't just with the dead."

Abu Illyas tsks and paces Layala's room in his house. "You should leave her here," he says, eyeing me coolly.

"I wouldn't want to move her home when she's so sick." I chew on my lip, thinking about Kamuna. She expects to speak to Layala today, and I know it is wiser to give her what she wants when she wants it, if only to avoid making matters worse.

"I mean, *leave* her," he says.

I bite back stinging words. Instead, I get up from my daughter's side, and though I am a head shorter than Abu Illyas, I look him right in the eye when I say, "No."

He steps back, his face red, jaw tight. He stands taller than I've seen him stand in a while. "I know what's best for my granddaughter," he sputters, jabbing his finger into his chest.

"Marrying her off to the highest bidder isn't what's best for her, Sheikh Hamadi. It's what's best for *you*. I am her *mother*, and she and I will both decide what's best for her."

"Then why bring her here?" he says. "Why bring her to my house and leave her behind?"

I force my voice to sound even. "I brought her here because I know you will keep her safe." I pause, then make a decision."But I am taking her back home to be with me. She will sleep in her own bed tonight."

I turn back to my sleeping daughter and dab a wet cloth against her skin. "I know you love her, Sheikh Hamadi. But I am her mother, and she will live with me."

Abu Illyas says something so low under his breath that I'm not sure I heard right, but the chill down my back tells me I did.

"She can't go home if her mother is dead."

I keep my mouth shut and continue pressing a cool cloth against Layala's hot face. Her skin is flushed, and a light sheen sits closely against her skin. Abu Illyas's footsteps recede as he leaves the room, and Layala's eyelids flicker open as soon as he shuts the door.

"Hiyati, my darling," I say. "How are you feeling now?"

She sits up in bed and pulls the covers aside. "Well enough to leave this place." She's already reaching for her bag and slipping on her boots, though she is unsteady on her feet.

"Wait, Layl, why the rush?" I try to pull her back into bed, but she's headstrong and pulls out of my grasp. "You're still running a fever and it's chilly outside. You'll catch your dea—"

"I'd rather catch my death in the cold than stay here another hour."

"But you love being at your jido's. Layl, tell me, what's happened?"

"Jido," she says. "He's been giving me a new dress each night now and parading me in front of those rich buffoons he calls friends and business partners. It's only this fever that's been a blessing, because he sent me right to bed when he realized I wasn't feeling well."

I pull her in for a hug, brushing her hair with my fingers. "He just wants what he thinks is best for you."

"Well, maman, like you said, you and I will decide that, not him."

"Your jido loves you, Layl. You know that." *Illyas would want me to tell her that.*

"I know, but he has an odd way of showing it. He's too . . ." She makes a gesture like she's choking someone. "I can see why baba left as soon as he could."

"No, Layl, stop. Don't say that. Your father never left home; he stayed under his father's roof until you were born."

"But he didn't spend much time here, did he? Jido said that once. He said he hopes I'd spend more time with him than his own son ever did. That's why I visit him, you know, because he's lonely." Her face melts at the thought. "And I think he's afraid of dying alone in this house."

Her skin is too warm from the fever as I cup her cheek in my palm. "You're doing a good thing, Layl. He loves you, and he cares for you. You *should* spend time with your grandfather." I kiss the top of her head and take her bag from her hand.

"What is it, maman?" she asks.

I sigh and raise my eyes to the blue painted ceiling. I trace the gold paint with my eyes before I reply. "There's someone I want you to meet."

Her eyes light up. "Who?"

"That woman, she spoke to you the day the men came. She has some questions to ask."

Layala's gaze narrows at me. "What questions?"

I don't answer her, but instead say, "You know of a jinn boy, Rami." I don't ask, but tell her.

Layala's cheeks redden, and she sinks back onto the bed. "He was sick, and I gave him some herbs. I've been checking up on him, you know, just to make sure he's fine."

Her cheeks glow a brighter red that isn't from the fever.

"I see. And what do you know about this boy?"

85

"Not much. I know he's jinn, or part jinn. But that confused me because, maman, didn't you tell me most jinns are dead or imprisoned?"

"Yes, Layl, I did. I thought the remaining ones were scattered across the earth, more in hiding than anything. But maybe I've been wrong all this time."

"Mmm," she says, chewing her lip like she does when she's thinking. "He said his parents are dead, and he had three younger siblings, but they all died, too. I don't know how, though. And he said he came from some village where there are other jinns."

"Why didn't you tell me this before?"

She shrugs and picks at the threads of her blanket.

"I worry about you, about you falling with child from some boy who won't stay around to care for you. Or someone hurting you, like those village boys. You need to tell me these things, Layl."

"Baba stuck around."

"Your father and I . . . well, we were soulmates, I think. Most people, even if they're in love, aren't."

Layala doesn't say anything for a few breaths. "I don't think this boy is my soulmate, maman. But there's something *off* about him."

My breath hitches in my throat. "*Off?*"

"I can't put my finger on it. I've been trying to figure him out, but he's tougher than a chestnut and I can't seem to crack him."

"Even a chestnut will crack under some heat," I say. "I'd tell you to stay away from him, but I know you won't listen." I half-smile, even as I sigh.

Layala laughs. "I'm only stubborn because you are."

"The one trait I'd have preferred *not* to pass on."

She moves toward the door. "I will feel better if you tell me more of that story you started, maman. About you and baba and the jinns."

86

I follow her out the door, shifting the weight of her bag over my shoulder. Her skin is flushed, but she is walking well. I consider asking the sheikh for a carriage, but decide not to.

"Tell your jido goodbye, Layl, before we leave."

She pouts, but goes off to find her grandfather. I wait by the door for her, the manservant glaring at me. But I don't move until I see Layala again, and we turn our backs on the house.

"Are you sure you are well enough to walk?" I ask as we step out into the cold air.

"I feel well enough to walk," Layala says. She stumbles forward, then catches herself. A guard darts out for her, but she waves his hand away. "I have a fever, not broken legs," she says with a smile.

The guard takes a step back, but his hand stays halfway out, ready to catch her if she stumbles again. But Layala doesn't, and I walk beside her. I match my pace to hers, and it takes twice the time to get home with all the breaks she needs.

"Well, where did I end last time?" I say, as we step onto the path leading to town. "Ah, yes, the babe and its mother were spared from imprisonment."

The babe's father begged the child to be spared. "She's not yet born," he told his father.

"She? Our men do not produce girls. They make boys."

"Nadine and I feel it's a girl. And a girl is no less than a boy, baba."

The sheikh laughed, shaking his head at what he considered his son's foolishness. "A girl will give you future heirs, but the boy is the heir. Their worth is not the same."

The man stood against his father, man to man now, rather than son to father. "Sheikh Hamadi, spare the life of my child and her mother, or you will lose me."

"Lose you?" the sheikh said, fear stabbing his heart at the thought of losing his only son. His only child. "How could you say such a thing?"

"Speaking as a father, to a father, I beg you, spare my child and her mother. Do what you will to me, but spare them."

The sheikh was angry, not used to being commanded or having things demanded of him. But he gave in to his son and spared the mother and the child.

Until, that is, the babe was born.

It was a girl, and the son insisted on giving her a jinn name. The sheikh grew furious, demanding the child's name be changed to something respectable, a human name. The mother and son refused, and they named their newborn daughter, Layala. Of the night.

The three lived in the sheikh's house, but they lived in fear. More and more jinns were being slaughtered or imprisoned, and the babe's mother knew her time was coming.

So, they stole into the night, wrapping their months-old daughter in warmth and keeping off well-trodden paths. They reached as far as seven villages away before the sheikh's men caught them and forced them to return.

They did, and the sheikh promised no retribution.

But the mother knew better. Maybe it was her jinn magic, or maybe it was a new mother's intuition, but she knew a storm was brewing.

And brew it did.

The sheikh imprisoned the mother's family, leaving her alone with just her child and her child's father. And then the sheikh turned on the mother.

Her child could be weaned, he said. What need for a mother was there? He knew he couldn't kill her, for his son would slay any who harmed her. But she was Hakawati, the last one, for he had imprisoned the one before her, and he knew her work was important. Instead of killing her, he imprisoned her. He used not metal, but wood, to keep her bound to the trees, to the cabin in the woods.

The mother could not leave the cabin, not three steps from it. Not at first. But as she grew into her jinn powers, she could go another step further each day, until weeks passed and she could step into the forest to gather herbs and mushrooms to feed her family.

Then the sheikh made a mistake: he took the daughter away from her parents and demanded he raise her away from jinn magic.

The parents fought hard to steal their child back, but the sheikh was powerful, with men beside and behind him. None could stand against him and win.

The son said he would die without his child, but the sheikh did not listen. The son demanded the return of his only daughter or he would drink a vial of poisoned herbs and take her with him.

The sheikh did not believe the son. He kept the daughter hidden away. The parents begged and pleaded, but the sheikh would not budge.

The son then forged a plan with his love, the jinn. She could pass the dead along, yes, but she could raise them too, as Hakawati. But, she warned him, she was still new to her powers, and there was no guarantee.

The son argued that there was no guarantee they'd ever get their daughter back, and dire situations called for dire measures.

Together, they planned; they planned he would drink poisoned herbs before the sheikh. He would die, and the jinn would promise to bring back the son to life if the sheikh returned their daughter.

They both knew she would bring him back from the dead even if their daughter was not returned. But they wagered the sheikh would be too distraught to consider that.

And so, they planned and they executed.

But the execution went wrong.

The son drank the poison, and he died, frothing at the mouth and in convulsions, as his father watched. The jinn demanded the return of her daughter—in exchange for bringing the son's life back.

The sheikh acquiesced, and the babe was returned to her mother's arms. The jinn, though she was powerful, was too green in her magic. She could not bring the body back, but she could hold the soul in death, to keep it from passing on to Jahannam, the realm of eternal suffering.

At first, the son visited the sheikh, spending scarce minutes a few mornings of the week with his father. But as time passed, he grew angry at the man who had raised him, who had taken his love's freedom and his daughter from him.

The sheikh begged the jinn to bring his son back to him, even if just for a minute each week. But the son refused, and the sheikh grew bitter. He regretted not killing the jinn, but knew he couldn't dare, not with the babe still young and his son still angry.

And so, he left them on their own in the little cabin in the woods with a half-jinn for a granddaughter and a dead son who refused to forgive him.

Layala doesn't say a word for a good minute. But when I touch her face, it is hot and wet.

"Layl," I say. "Layl. It's just a story."

"But it's *your* story. *Our* story."

"Everyone's life is a story, Layl."

"But this one is cruel. And it's because of jido."

"No, Layl. Your grandfather, he's . . . in pain. I think he's always been since your *tita*, your grandmother, died. And people in pain either grow bigger hearts to bring more love in to replace the pain, or their hearts shrink to protect themselves from more pain." *I don't tell her that I'd have slit his throat years ago given the chance, to prevent the murder and imprisonment of my kind. But I didn't; for love of her father, I didn't. And I regret it every day. The only thing stilling my hand now is her.*

"I think jido's heart shrunk. I'm not even sure he *has* a heart."

"Oh, Layl," I say, kissing the top of her head. "*You* are his heart. And don't forget that. Don't turn yourself away from him because you're angry at something that happened in the past. Keep your heart open to him; he needs you."

"How are you not angry at him?"

"I am, Layl. But what good is that anger when I have you to think about?"

"What do you mean?" Her tone is airy like a cloud and, in that moment, I envy her youthful ignorance.

"You, Layl, you are my moon, my sun, the earth at my feet, the sky above my head, the air in my lungs. If I hurt your grandfather, I hurt you. And I could never do that."

"But—"

"Shh," I say, and rest a finger against her lips. "I am angry, yes. I hate him, yes. But anger and hate consume the one who carries them, not the one they're meant for. Remember that, Layl, and carry it to your grave."

Layala sniffles, but then nods against my chest. "You're right, maman."

"It's been a long time since I heard you say that, kushtbani."

She snorts, rolls her eyes, then snuggles in against my side, even as we walk. "I promise I won't make it a habit."

14

As soon as we reach home, I tuck Layala in bed before I even remove my cloak or start the fire. She doesn't argue as I slip off her shoes, untie her hair from its messy braid, and set a glass of water beside her bed.

"Maman?" she says, her wrist limp as her hand hangs over the edge of her bed.

"Yes, hiyati?"

"You'll never leave me like baba left us, will you?"

Her words are slurred, and I see the fever rising higher in her cheeks. I ready a bowl of cool water and clean cloths and mix her a brew of elderflower and white willow bark to bring down the body's heat.

"Never, hiyati," I say.

"And you won't marry me off to some man I don't love?"

"No, never, hiyati. You will have your choice when you are of the right age."

"Mmm," she hums, and then she's asleep, though her breath is ragged and her skin is hot to the touch. I bring water up to her lips, tilting her head forward so that at least her mouth won't dry out. Is this death's doing? Spiting me by threatening my child's life? A panic seizes me, and I force my hand to steady and my breath to settle.

This is not Kamuna's doing. This is a simple fever, one any child would catch. A fever, and nothing more.

But fear nags at me, chasing every thought I have, even as I prepare more elderflower tea for Layl and try to help her drink it.

The fever keeps rising, and my worry with it. I spend the day trying to cool down her skin, pressing wet cloths to her face and arms and neck.

But even then, her skin burns, and she yells out in her sleep. "Help me! Help me!"

"Oh, hiyati, I'm here," I say, but she doesn't hear me, though I'm right beside her, dabbing at her hot face.

"Help me! Water!" she screams.

I tilt her head forward, helping her drink water, but she splutters as she tries to gulp it, and next thing, she's choking and vomiting all over her blanket.

Oh, Illyas, I wish you were here now, alive, with us.

But I've gotten used to banishing these thoughts over the years.

"Your fever will burn your brain," I tell Layala as she screams out once more. I rush outside to the old leaning shed behind the house, stumbling over roots and stones along the path in my hurry.

I have garden and graveyard tools in there, old cans, seeds wrapped in packets, and even animal bones still with marrow in them.

But at the back is an old tin tub that I drag out to the front of the house. The cottage is too small for the bath, so I leave it in the front and run to pump well water into buckets to fill the tub.

When the tub is filled a few inches, I see a figure rounding the path up to the cottage.

Kamuna.

"She can't talk now," I tell her, trying to wave her off. I see anger dance across her face. "Please, come back another day. I'm sorry," I add, forcing softness into my voice, hoping to soothe her anger.

She glances over my shoulder and into the house.

"She has a bad fever," I say.

"Move, Hakawati," she demands and slips past me into the house.

She's hovering over Layala when I dash in after her. She has a hand pressed against my daughter's forehead.

"A shame," she says. "Her magic is quite strong. I knew I sensed it."

"Move away from her," I say and slap Kamuna's hand. I pull at Layala's limp body and hold her to my chest. "Take her legs," I tell Kamuna. "I need to cool her body."

She helps me carry Layala outside to the metal tub. We sit her against it, her voice murmuring something I can't make out.

"Do you have a second bucket?" Kamuna asks, already grabbing the one I was using. She rushes to the well, pumping water into the bucket and dashing to pour it into the tub.

"Yes, yes, in the shed," I say, my feet already taking me there.

We spend the next quarter hour filling buckets and the tub with cold well water, each of us rushing past the other from the well to the tub and back.

"Set her down gently," I say. "The cold will be a shock."

We ease her in, feet first, then back, and arms. Layala yells out and fights us, trying to pull herself out of the tub.

"Layl, hiyati," I say, pulling her back down into the tub. "Your body is burning up."

But she screams again, yelling that I'm trying to drown her. She's screaming and thrashing against our hold.

Blue, my baby is blue, and pale, and limp. Her lips are blue, and her eyes are shut. She feels at once heavy and weightless. Her tiny lungs are filled with pond water.

I banish the memory of Layl as a baby, even as she screams I'm drowning her—that she's drowning once again.

"You're not drowning, Layl," I say.

"She's delirious," Kamuna says. She runs back into the house and hurries back with an empty glass. She fills it with fresh well water and brings it to Layala's lips. Layala swipes at her and knocks the glass out of her hand.

I take the glass and try to get her to drink a few sips. "Layl, please," I say. "Ya hiyati, drink a bit." She does, then collapses back into the tub, her teeth chattering.

"Move," Kamuna commands and leans over the tub.

Her own skin is blue, I notice, and mottled, as if rotting from the inside out. But she runs her hands over Layala's shivering body.

I run inside the house and pull at jars of herbs. I mix them together as I mash other plants, creating a stronger brew than flower and bark that brings down fever. When I return, Kamuna is humming to Layala, as if she were her mother and Layala her sick baby. I watch for just a breath, feeling a tenderness grow in my heart before I hurry toward them.

"She needs to drink this," I say, and press the green-brown brew to Layala's lips.

Layala splutters and spits out the drink, but I force her mouth again to the cup.

"Let me," Kamuna offers and takes the glass. "You go rest for a moment."

"I'm not leaving you alone with my child."

"I won't kill her," she says, but the glint in her eyes sends my blood cold.

"No," I say, taking the glass back from her. "You've done enough."

I don't know how much time has passed between sinking Layala in the tub, pulling her out, and carrying her back inside. Kamuna doesn't lift a finger again to help, and just as well, but she keeps to a chair, watching us. I ignore her between pressing cool cloths to Layala's skin and forcing some water down her throat.

I'm nodding off when Layala stirs. "Mmm. Maman?"

"I'm here, hiyati, right here," I say, and press a cool cloth against her skin.

"I'm feeling a bit better," she says.

Kamuna clears her throat and elbows me out of the way. She hovers both hands above Layala's head and runs her fingers down her body.

"Maman, I'm cold," Layala says.

Kamuna then presses her palms into Layala's chest, and I feel warmth radiate from both of them, like a fire that presses in a bit too close for comfort.

"I have healed her," Death says as she steps away from Layala's cot.

Layala sits up, her eyes darting between Kamuna and me.

"Now, girl," Kamuna says, "we can have that talk I've been meaning to have." She nestles on the edge of Layala's cot, helping my daughter sit up.

"Layl," I say, "you need your rest." I shoot a pointed glance at Kamuna.

"She is well," Death says. "Look at her. The picture of life and health."

"I feel fine, maman," Layala says. "Just a bit thirsty."

I fetch her a cup of water, keeping both eyes and ears on the two of them.

"Tell me, girl, what is it you want to do with your life?" Kamuna asks.

I give Layl the water, and she gulps it down before she answers. I lean forward, watching Layala's face closely, eager to hear her every word. *I want to know her. I want to know her thoughts. Talk to me Layl, the way you used to.*

"I want to *do* things. Lots of things. I want to see the world, meet people. I want to be able to say I've lived."

"And what if I told you your life isn't your own?"

"Kamuna," I say, but it's too late. Layala's eyes narrow at the both of us.

"What do you mean?" she asks.

"You died," Kamuna says, and my heart splinters.

"When you were a baby," I add hastily. "I brought you back to life. Your father—"

"I never knew that," Layl breaks in, her eyes wandering over Kamuna's face.

"Now you do," Death says. "And you owe me a favor."

"Kamuna, you said—"

"Oh, hush, Hakawati," she snaps. "I'm speaking to the girl."

"Layala. Her name is—"

But Kamuna waves me off.

"I allowed your mother to raise you," Death says. "Your life is mine, girl, and I have come to retrieve it."

Layala's eyes widen, and she darts her gaze between Death and me and back again. "Am I to die?"

"Yes," Kamuna says, just as I say, "No."

My daughter bunches her blanket closer around her as if that could protect her. Her throat rises and falls as she swallows several times.

"Drink," I tell her, handing her another glass of water. She takes the cup from me but doesn't drink. She only stares at Kamuna like a rabbit caught in a hunter's trap.

"Please," she says, and her voice is so low I can barely make out the word.

"That is the way of life and of death," Kamuna says. "All things borrowed must be returned. All favors owed must be paid."

"*I* owe you the favor," I say. "Not my daughter."

"Your daughter *is* your favor, Hakawati," Kamuna says, rising to her feet. "I'll claim her in three days."

"No."

"What?" Death blinks once, then laughs. "Oh, Hakawati, what makes you think—"

"I offer myself."

"You're not death-touched."

"Kill me, then resurrect me."

"That is not how it works, Hakawati. You know this."

I don't care. I don't care. I don't care. All I want is to keep Layala from this fate, this sure death. No matter what Kamuna says.

"Yes, yes, it will work. Kill me, resurrect me, as many times as you need to."

Kamuna gives a dry laugh. "Even if that would work, I cannot raise you without a willing sacrifice. I need souls, bodies, to sacrifice in exchange for your life. I can't simply—"

"You are *Death* itself. You are the realm made flesh. You *can.*"

"I cannot!"

The force of her words throws me back.

She takes a step toward me, her face twisted in anger. "Do you think my own child, my Sayil, would still be dead if I could simply exchange her life for another's? I did not make the rules of my realm, I inherited them, and I have no choice but to obey them."

"You can," I say. "You can find a way."

Kamuna throws her hands in the air. "Even if I could resurrect you, even if your magic was able to handle taking my place as Death, then what? You couldn't visit your daughter; she couldn't visit you."

"She would be *alive.*"

"And you would be alone."

"I would sacrifice myself for her to live."

"Maman, no," Layala says, slipping out of bed now. She comes to stand beside me. "I will do it," she says.

"No, Layala, you will not," I argue and gently force her behind me.

"Maman! I said I will do it. I wasn't even meant to be alive now if it weren't for what you and Death did. I would be dead today, maman."

"Yes, you would," Kamuna says. "And here I am offering you three more days. You have had thirteen more years than you were meant to live. That is more than my daughter got when she died at just about your age now, Layala." Kamuna's chest is heaving, her face twisted in anger.

"Why now?" I ask. "Why have you come for her now? Why is your soul seed sick *now?*"

"My time has come, Hakawati, and frankly, I couldn't be happier."

"Happier?" I gawk at her. "You're taking my child's life—"

"I *gave* her life, remember. I am taking what I gave."

"Take it later! Take it years and years and years from now!"

"Without me, you wouldn't have a child," Kamuna points out. "I should have let her stay dead, but I showed you mercy and gave you your child back. Without me, she'd have rotted in her grave years ago instead of living, breathing, right beside you. You had a chance to be a mother. Let me have my chance and return to *my* child."

"Please, Kamuna, leave Layala alone."

"I cannot!" she screams back. "I am dying! And Death itself cannot live without a ruler's magic to keep it in place."

"Find someone else!"

"There is no other, Hakawati! There is no other."

"I will do it, maman," Layala says softly.

"See? The girl is willing," Kamuna says.

"I want my child to have known love and have tasted all that life has to offer. She's seen barely more than a dozen turnings of the sun." I soften my voice and reach my hands out a bit toward Death, not quite touching, but close. "Please," I whisper. "Make me the next Death but return Layala her life."

Her face softens a bit, and a finger twitches.

I whisper breathlessly. "From one mother to another, let me make a mother's sacrifice and give my life for my child's."

Kamuna sucks air through her teeth, as if considering what I'm saying.

Then her face hardens, and she searches mine with her dark eyes. I try to make my expression as open as possible. *There is no guile here, only grief.* I will her to recognize that.

"It won't work, Hakawati."

"What if I can heal your soul seed?" I blurt.

Kamuna blinks. "How?"

"I don't know. But what if I could?"

She sighs. "Truly, Hakawati, I am ready to die. I am ready to pass on to Mote and pass my daughter on with me. I want to be with her again."

I pause. "Pass your daughter on? I thought she died—"

Kamuna interrupts. "I preserved her soul seed and body in death's holding waters, in case I could ever find a willing sacrifice to raise her with." Her voice drops. "But I never could."

My thoughts are clotted, and I can't think straight. "There has to be a way."

"There is not, Hakawati," Kamuna says, her voice gentler than I've ever heard it. "I am sorry. But my time has come, and your daughter's, too. You have three days."

A knock sounds at the door.

"Who could that be now!" I scream out in exasperation.

I fling open the door and find Rami standing there, a bag slung over his shoulder.

"Jinn!" Kamuna shrieks, pushing past me. "Go from here. You're not welcome."

He glances between us. "What is going on?" he asks, his eyes wide, like a doe's. He's flicking his gaze between Kamuna, me, and Layala.

"Rami!" Layala says.

"Layl? Are you alright?"

Her chin quivers, but she nods. "It's good you came by. I'll be gone in three days."

"Gone? Where?"

"Nowhere," Kamuna and I say at the same time.

"It doesn't concern you," I add.

"Death," Layala cuts in. "I am to die in three days and take over as Death."

Rami blinks and stumbles back. "What?"

"Oh, hush," Kamuna says to him. "I've had enough of you."

"Take your place as Death?" he says to Kamuna. "When I myself have asked countless times to take on your mantle?"

"You've what!" I whip around to face Kamuna. "You have a willing soul here to take your mantle, and you would kill my child instead?"

I strangle the urge to rush at her, to stab her, to choke her, to harm her in some way and get her out of our lives.

"Yes," Kamuna says. "He is not worthy."

I ignore her. "Are *you* death-touched?" I ask Rami.

"Yes. I died as a child, and my mother had me resurrected."

Kamuna doesn't meet my gaze.

"Take him," I say. "Take him and leave my child alone."

"No."

"But I don't understand," I say. "He is willing."

"He killed my child! He killed my Sayil! And you expect me to simply hand him the keys to my realm as some favor?"

"Then make it be his atonement! He will die to bring Sayil back! It won't be a favor, it would be an offering. You get what you want, and he gets what he wants, and Layala isn't harmed in any of it."

"He killed my child, Hakawati. He pushed her in a river, and she drowned."

"It was an accident," Rami insists. "And it was so many moons ago, so many years have passed."

"And none of them with my Sayil alive during any of it," Kamuna says. "Because of you." She jabs her finger into his chest.

"Would you be a sacrifice?" I say to Rami. "To raise Sayil."

"But my family . . ."

"Is dead to you. Your own mother wouldn't lift a finger to help you. You are alone in this world, Rami. You can't even show your face to people or they would kill you. You are also on borrowed time," Kamuna says.

"I-I don't want . . ." Rami stutters.

Kamuna snorts. "He thinks of no one but himself. But, Hakawati, even if you raised Sayil, then what? I would still have to pass my mantle to someone."

It hits her then. She realizes what I intended all along.

"You want me to pass my mantle on to her."

I nod. "Sayil can take your place, and I could keep your soul so that you do not go past the gates of Mote. You and your daughter would be reunited, even if in death."

Kamuna purses her lips, then glances at Rami.

"You could do that?" she asks me.

"I could try, yes, if I had a willing sacrifice to raise Sayil with."

"I won't do it," Rami says. "I will not die—"

"I will raise your family," Kamuna says, interrupting.

"You said you couldn't," Rami begins.

"I lied."

He narrows his eyes at her. "You're lying now."

"Not at all," Death says. "Give me one of them. I will raise them from their clay prison."

"But you would need a sacrifice."

"Their souls are intact, no? They are still alive, only imprisoned. Only the dead need true resurrection and a sacrifice."

Rami sniffs. "All this time, you could have raised my family, and yet you didn't."

"Yes."

He shrugs. "Why would I help you now?" He shakes his head and turns away, already moving out the door.

"You will help now," Death says, "because that is the only way to get what you want. You have spent a lifetime trying to raise your father, your cousins, your siblings, and you have failed. I am giving you the chance to do so now."

"I would die," he says, but his eyes show cunning. "I would die, but they would live," he mutters, more to himself.

"And Sayil would be resurrected," I say. "You could redeem yourself, your life for hers."

Rami blinks and takes a step back.

"You can't do this to him," Layala says, as if unfreezing from the moment. "It is my time to die, not his." But her voice is weak; she's shivering on her feet.

He eyes Layala, who's standing with her arms hugging her body. But her head is high and her eyes bore right into Rami's.

"Stay out of this, Layl," he says.

He looks at me now. "I came by to see you, Hakawati, to see if you would reconsider my request."

I shake my head. "If I could, I would have done so already."

He sets his bag down now, clay clinking inside, and pulls out one figurine.

"Do it," he says to Kamuna. "Raise my father."

Death takes the small clay figure of a man from him and inspects it. "Handsome," she says finally, then sets it down at her feet. She bends at the waist and presses her palms against the figurine, enveloping it. Her eyes flutter, and she chants in a language I am sure has never been human.

And then she steps back. The figurine topples over and my heart clenches, expecting the clay to shatter into pieces.

Instead, it stretches and widens, as dough does when a rolling pin is taken to it.

"There," Kamuna says. "See what a little earth magic can do?"

A man stands before us, his hair tipped in fire, his body glazed in ash. His skin is the color of the earth after a spring rain, and his eyes are the same shade of green as the ivy clinging to my cottage walls.

"Baba?" Rami whispers, stretching out his hand to his father. His father blinks once, twice, and stumbles forward, his son catching him.

"Sit, sit," I say, and Layala runs to get a chair for the man.

"Rami," the man croaks, and as soon as his body touches the wood of the chair, he turns to clay again.

Kamuna snatches the figurine and pockets it.

"No!" Rami screams and lunges for her. "Please, that was my father, please." His voice quivers, and he looks as if ready to drop to his knees and beg.

But she shoves him back and turns her body away from him. "You've seen what my magic can do."

"Raise him back!" Rami pleads. He's crying now, tears streaming down his face. He's on his knees before Kamuna, reaching out for the skim of her cloak. "I have no one left," he says. "Bring him back to me."

"Not until Sayil is warm and alive in my arms," Kamuna answers coldly. "I will keep your father for safekeeping until then."

She raises an eyebrow at Rami as he eyes the pocket his father is in, and for a breath, I think he is going to try to reach for it.

But he doesn't. Instead, he rises to his feet. He lifts his head, his chin straight and proud. "I will do it, for my family. But I will need a day."

"A day for what, jinn?" Kamuna asks.

"Let him be," I say, relief flooding me. Layala is going to live. *Layala is going to live. My daughter will live.*

Kamuna stares at Rami, then frowns. "One day."

Rami bows his head, then slings his bag over his shoulder. "Shukran," he says. "My family means more to me than anything."

The moment he disappears from our view, Kamuna shakes her head. "I don't trust him as far as I can spit." She turns her gaze to me. "You. You have work to do."

15

KAMUNA LEAVES, AND LAYALA CURLS up before the fire, blanket around her shoulders.

"I don't want to die," she says, not looking at me. "But I don't think Rami should die, either."

"He's made his choice, Layl."

She turns to look back at me. "Has he? Or was he forced into a choice because I'm too cowardly to accept my fate?"

"No. You are not a coward. You are young, and strong, and healthy, and worthy of the life you have."

"I should be dead."

"You should be nothing but what you are now. Alive."

Layala turns back to the fire. "I shouldn't be alive. I died thirteen years ago."

"And you were brought back, Layl," I plead, my voice rising desperately. I settle in beside her and pull her in to me. But she leans away and doesn't look me in the eye.

"It's not fair."

"What's not fair, Layl?"

Her eyes flick up to mine, rimmed in red. "It's not fair. Entire families slaughtered in their beds, in their homes, even their *palaces*, or imprisoned. And I was resurrected because my mother is Hakawati."

"That is life, Layl. The lucky and the unlucky walk the earth just the same."

"I could—could I go with you?" she suggests. "Into death, help you heal the soul seed?"

"You could do a lot of things, but not all of them would be prudent."

"You need me," she says. "To watch out for you. I'm old enough, maman."

I gently touch her cheek but shake my head. "I love how you want to be by my side, but this is my job, as Hakawati, to fix. Not yours."

"But when you die . . ." She flinches at the thought. "When you die, there's no one to take your Hakawati role. I'm not trained for it, but I could be."

"Oh, hiyati, I wish. You'd make a great one. But you have human blood," I say as gently as I can. "You need full jinn magic to be a hakawati."

Something flashes across her face, a glint in her eyes and a setting of her mouth I've never seen before.

"You have a role, a *purpose* in life. What do I have?"

My breath hitches in my throat at the force of her words. "You have the freedom to be *anything* you want to be, Layl. That is a greater gift than you think," I say.

"I want to be Hakawati. I want to be like you."

"Layl," I say. "You have the world in your hand. You're young and smart and fiery. And I love that about you. You have your own role in life, I promise you that. But yours is different from mine, which is different from the next person." I draw her in close so I can plait her hair. "You are the most important, greatest gift of my life. I can't let anything happen to you."

She hangs her head and I tug at the plait to tighten it. "I wish . . . Couldn't you teach me your magic? Can't you show me how to do—"

I sigh, pulling her into my side. "It doesn't work like that. You are either born with magic or you are not."

"Maybe my magic is late, or-or it's different than yours, or . . ." Her voice strains, searching, latching onto any answer. "Death thinks I have—"

I interrupt her. "Half jinns rarely have magic, or strong magic, at least. Besides, being human is its own kind of magic." *And having no magic gives you a simpler life, hiyati. The only one I want for you.*

Her frown settles deeper and I regret saying anything.

I pause, turning her to look at me. "It's not easy, my job. You only see the good parts, the safe parts, the storytelling, the passing on of souls. But death is not a joke. Death is frightening and dangerous. Even if eating a seed could let you in, I would still forbid it."

She says nothing, but glances away. "Fine," she says. "I still don't think it's fair."

I lay a hand on her shoulder. "You have it easy, Layl. Keep it that way. And I'm sorry," I add. "I know you want to help."

"I don't just want to *help*. I want to *be*. To be something, to be a jinn, to be magical, to have powers."

"Layl, what you want isn't magic. It's to feel powerful or special, no?"

She shrugs but doesn't say anything.

"You are already special to me."

"No. No, maman, that's not it. I want . . ." She forces a breath out of her mouth as she stares up at the sky. "I want to *do*, to *be*. You have a job, an important one, and I want that."

"You will have that, Layl, all that and more. Give yourself time. You are still so young."

"I'm not much younger than you were when you had me."

"And I was too young then."

"But you did it. You were given the choice, and you took it."

I laugh. "Oh, Layl, it wasn't much of a choice. I'm glad I have you, and I'm glad you're my daughter, but if I had waited even a few years—"

"That's not the point," she says, cutting me off. "You had a *chance* and you made it work. That's all I need, a chance. I promise you, I can do it. I'll help you. I'll do anything you want. But why not let me *try?*"

Her eyes are wide and pleading, and they're brimming with tears. I cradle her to my chest, trying to pass every ounce of love I have for her through our skin.

"Layl, if I let you try, you will be dead."

"I will be alive in the greatest way possible. I would *be* Death."

"You would be dead, no matter which way you look at it."

"Kamuna can leave death. We've seen her, she's been here."

"Kamuna has been Death for more moons than anyone we know or knew has been alive. Kamuna is . . . She is beyond time; of it, yes, but beyond it. She has had to sacrifice much to become Death. She wasn't always able to leave her realm."

When she doesn't answer, I say, "How about I tell you a story?"

Still, she doesn't reply, but as I start the story, she sits up a bit straighter and I can tell she's listening.

There was once a boy and a girl, born of the same womb, on the same day. The boy was named Luck, and the girl was named Fate. Each was beautiful—Luck with his hair the color of a setting sun; Fate with her eyes as dark as the deepest sea.

The two were inseparable. Always could they be found with hands held tight, moving through life as if they shared the same arms and the same legs.

And so, it went on, until the boy's shoulders and the girl's hips began to widen.

They stopped holding hands. Instead of the same path into the town market every morning, they now went different ways. Luck would take the left, and Fate, the right.

Their parents fretted that an animal or a bandit would seize on one of them alone and begged them to stay together.

But Luck and Fate were growing older and growing apart. They bickered over little things, like who got more creamed ice than the other or who had more sugar sprinkled over their fried dough.

Now, their parents grew angry at how stubborn and selfish their children were becoming.

One morning, Luck and Fate argued over who was more popular with their friends. Luck claimed their friends admired his strength and speed, and how well he could shoot with an arrow. Fate argued that, no, their friends preferred her beautiful voice and pretty face and her quick wit.

The two left their house, still arguing over who their friends preferred. They took the same path until it forked, and because they were still lost in their silliness, they continued on the same path rather than going their separate ways.

Because they were busy bickering, they didn't notice the bear lumbering toward them. It was a cub, but where there's a cub, there's a mother bear. And mother bears are ferocious.

Fate nearly walked into the cub, screaming when she saw it just paces away from her. Luck froze, and all the strength and speed he claimed he had trickled out of his limbs, and he dropped to the ground.

Fate screamed at him to get up and to run, but Luck sat there, frozen, staring at something beyond the cub. When Fate looked, she saw the mother bear—large, black, her jaws wide open to reveal sharp teeth.

"Luck!" Fate yelled, pulling at her brother's shoulder. "Get up!"

But Luck was frozen in fear, even as the bear charged at them.

Layala coughs and I realize she is shivering. I tuck the blanket tighter around her, layering her with a second.

"What happened?" she asks. "Did the bear kill them?"

"Ah, yes, Luck and Fate. Let's see."

The mother bear charged at them, and just at the last breath, Luck's limbs unfroze. He grabbed his sister's hand and pulled her away, but though he was fast, Fate was a bit slower. She stumbled, screaming, as the bear came rushing at her.

Luck threw himself over his sister to protect her from the bear's jaws. The beast ripped into his back, tearing off a piece of flesh.

Fate screamed, shoving her brother off her and grabbing a stick to stab the bear in the eye. But this only made it angrier, and with a swipe of her claws, she slit open Fate's belly.

Luck and Fate lay down covered in each other's blood, bleeding out into the woods. In their final breaths, they took each other's hands and held tight. When trappers found them two days later, their bodies were frozen, their hands interlocked, just as when they were born.

"They were upset with themselves for arguing over silly things," I say. "They even argued about it in death, until they realized what they were doing and laughed about it."

Layala's eyebrows flew up. "You know them?"

"Eh," I say. "I helped write their story to pay Mote's gate-keeper with."

"So, they're *real*?" she asks, sitting up straighter.

I nod. "Most of my stories are, and the people in them. It's a shame about Luck and Fate, though. So young and really quite pretty, the both of them. But as *luck* would have it, their *fate* was to die as they were born: together."

Layala cracks a smile at my joke of sorts.

"Ah, it's been a while since anyone thought I was funny," I say, chuckling more to myself than to her.

Layala yawns and draws her knees up to her chest.

"I think tonight, we should sleep outside. Under the stars, like we used to."

As many stars as there are in the sky, that is how many breaths I will love you for, Illyas once told me, when we were young, before Layala was born. I smile at the memory, even as my heart yearns to hear his voice beside me again.

I pull my blanket off my cot and wrap it around me. In the corner of the cottage, a few stone steps lead up to a flat door built into the roof. I draw the bolt lock and push the wooden door up and set it down. Outside on my flat roof, it's chilly, and the wind blows steady around me. The trees sway, but the sky is clear. Layala follows after me, dragging her blankets behind her.

Illyas and I used to lay under the stars, counting them and drawing out the constellations. I would tell him stories about the hunter and the huntress, the butcher and the cow, anything I could think of just to stay longer in his arms, at least until the rising sun chased us off, back to our parents' houses to pretend we had been asleep in our beds the whole night.

Thoughts swirl in my mind, even as I tuck Layala in on the mats on the roof and I settle in next to her. When I try to catch on one thought, it slips out of my grasp like a cold, writhing fish.

All will be well, all will be right in the end.

I pull my prayer beads from my pocket and repeat my prayer for Layl, over and over, until my eyelids feel as heavy as my heart.

Keep her safe.
Keep her happy.
Let her find good love.
Let her know peace.
Let her know her heart and mind.
Let her be.

Before I know it, my eyes shut and I'm asleep.

16

I WAKE AS THE SUN peeks through gray clouds. Layala is gone from beside me, but I can hear her in the cottage below, cups and plates clinking as she sets them on the table.

I lean over the roof's edge, looking for pomegranate seeds, but the ground is bare save for leaves, stones, and dirt, and our footprints from the day before.

"Not even one," I say to myself. Not even one seed, one soul to help pass through death. An emptiness flashes through me, like a part of my own soul is missing. To be willing to do work and have that taken from you . . . I shake my head to clear myself of the feeling.

But worry creeps back in. Without the dead passing into Mote, the Waiting Place in death can only hold so many souls. And when it becomes overrun, those souls spill back into life, without bodies, hungry to return to the lives they had before. And those desperate souls prey on whichever bodies they can find.

I find myself clutching the blanket tight against my chest, as if it could protect me from the hungry dead when they decide death isn't big enough for them and start forcing their way into life.

Cool, fat raindrops wash my face before they come pouring down over me. I gather up my blanket and head down into the house, shutting the door to the roof behind me to keep the rain from soaking through to our floor.

I have only one story of what happens to the hungry dead—one story my maman told me, when she was teaching me the responsibility a hakawati has, the *obligation* to be hakawati, even if unwilling. But I shove the story down my throat and swallow it into my stomach.

Layala's skin looks less feverish, less red and more of her normal healthy pink.

I bend over and touch my hand to her forehead. She's warm but she's cooler than she was yesterday.

"How are you feeling?"

"Better," she says and twists away from my touch. A pang shoots through my heart for her hurt, her confusion, even her anger. But she will understand one day, when she is older. She will understand and she will accept.

A few minutes later, the tea is brewing, olives and oil are laid out on the table, along with two-day old flatbread that's still fresh with herbs, and some jams and balls of cheese I was keeping on the windowsill to cure the past few weeks.

"I am going for a walk," Layala announces after she has eaten, and she doesn't wait for my reply. I let her go, knowing she needs time to be alone. When she leaves, I unlock the old trunk and bring out the small metal lamp filled with sloshing smoke.

I unstopper the bottle, rub the metal with my hand three times, and smoke curls out of its long open spout.

I'm sorry, maman. I know you are weary. But the dead aren't passing. If the dead do not pass, they will escape into life. Here, they'll steal bodies, wearing them and discarding them like the furs the fancier women in other towns do.

My maman's ephemeral body stands before me, her face gray and wispy. Still, a smile curls on her face, and she reaches a hand out to me. She's more unsteady on her feet than the last time I saw her; each time I release her from her prison, she's more faded, less of who she was and more smoke. My insides gnaw with guilt, but I need my maman.

I reach out my hands to her, but of course my flesh brushes through her smoke. The smile on her face drops, and she nods at the table and chairs.

"Hakawati," she greets.

"I know you prefer your rest," I say.

She smiles again. "It's always a joy to see my beautiful daughter." Her voice is weaker than before, and her face is strained, as if she's focusing all her energy on not fading into the air. The guilt rises again like bile in my throat, but I force it back.

"Ah, maman," I say, as she sits on a chair. She hovers an inch above the wood, more a pretense of sitting than anything. "I wish this was just a pleasure visit."

My mother's face darkens in worry. "What is it, hiyati? What's happened?"

"The dead," I say. "There haven't been any seeds, and death won't let me enter it."

My mother's shoulders tense, but then she's turned back at the table, drumming her fingers above it, as if she were as solid as the wood. "It's been a long time since that happened. I remember hearing of it in my great-great-great-grand-mother's time, when she was young, and her own grandmother was Hakawati. She was storyteller to a king who married her because of the stories she spun."

"How can I fix it?" I ask. "What can I do?"

"I don't know, Hakawati. But I do know a story."

17

MAMAN TELLS A STORY, AND I feel myself slipping into memories of my childhood. Of growing up in our jinn village, of courtyards and dances, of dinners and feasts. Of my mother sitting beside my father, the sheikh of our village, weaving stories with the Hakawatis of other tribes. Of *ouds* strumming songs, of calfskin drums and *qanuns* telling their own tales in music. I remember the sizzling of meat cooking over fires, of the smell of herbs and of tea brewing hot against cool nights. Everything that is now lost, stolen from us.

Her voice is warbling and hoarse, but she speaks with the conviction a dervish has of his dance.

Death was once a maiden. She was dark-haired, and dark-eyed, and her skin was as vibrant as the full moon.

She lived alone under the earth, part of it, yet separate. All things that died, be it animal or plant or human or jinn or efrit, or any creature that ever walked the earth or flew the sky or swam the sea, would rot, and their skins and bones would sink down to death.

Death spent her days cleaning up the rot, sweeping and collecting the sinew and teeth and hair that collected in her home. But she was growing tired of doing so.

The bodies were all made of Earth, which gave flesh and bone. The bodies were given souls made of Sky. Blood was brought to life by Fire and Sea.

And so, Death asked her friends, creatures of stone and sand and clay, water and foam and flame, breath and dirt. She asked them for their help.

Earth fashioned a being made of clay and sand and made golems.

Sea made a creature of salt and water and gave rise to marids.

Sky took air and cloud wisps and rain and made ghouls.

Fire took ash and smoke and made jinns.

But Death was not happy with these gifts. For after each one died, it made more mess, more work for her. And though jinns and golems, marids and ghouls helped collect the bodies, with Fire burning them, then reusing the ash to make more jinns, it wasn't enough.

And it wasn't enough because Death thought it all a waste. Beautiful bodies and beings, she claimed, should not be burned then refashioned. Each one should be given a soul that belonged once to that body, and to that body alone. And that soul should be given a chance to live long after the body was just a memory.

Then, Death did something her friends did not approve of.

She took jinns' gift of Fire and trained them in the art of gleaning the stories of souls, and then giving those stories back to the souls to remind them of the lives they lived in their bodies. She took a golem and appointed it as her gate-keeper to the realm of Mote and named him Mote after his appointed gate.

Those jinns became the Hakawati jinns, and for as long as they and Death have existed, they have been telling the stories of the dead.

But Death knew one day she would pay the price of going against her friends. For Death and her friends served not themselves or each other, but a greater power. One they had never seen, but had felt. This power was the source of all that ever came into being. It was thunder and lightning and light—and perhaps even life itself.

And Death felt that power growing stronger in her realm. That power kept pushing at her boundaries, getting in the way of souls leaving their bodies or reclaiming the souls of the newly dead.

Death grew angry, for souls were hers and hers alone. That was her right as Death. She added more gates in death, more gatekeepers, and appointed more Hakawati jinns so that there would be less time between the moment a body dies and their souls leave their bodies. Less time for that power to interfere.

Still, that power was stronger than Death and her friends combined, and souls slipped into its hands. But as more Hakawati jinn were trained and appointed, and more gate-keepers stood guard around Death's realm, fewer and fewer souls were caught by that power. One day, Death learned that the power was put to sleep in a cauldron of heated stone and sand, and covered with a layer of ash, and sealed over by the sky, and surrounded by the sea.

But Death was no fool, and she knew one day, that power would awaken. It would be hungry for new souls to give it more power, more strength. So, Death did some-thing: she put to sleep her own Hakawati. Not all, for she still needed them to tell the stories of the dead, but she put to sleep her most skilled, most powerful. And she did the same with all of her gatekeeepers until only the origi-nal, like Mote, were left.

"But maman," I say, "what does all this mean?"

"It means you must find a way to work with Death herself to heal whatever has gone ill."

"She told me her soul seed is sick. What does that mean?"

"It means, Hakawati, that you need to find Death's soul seed and heal it."

"But how do I do that?" I ask, my voice rising. "I'm *one* jinn."

"You will have to, Hakawati."

"But how do I heal a sick soul seed? When people are dying, their seeds rot before their body does. Kamuna—Death—she's dying. How would I stop that?"

"You are of the last of your kind who walks the earth as flesh and bone and not as smoke in a bottle. You must find a way to do your job."

"But maman . . ." I sound like a whining child, even to myself.

"Nado," she says, using her nickname for me. "Nadine. You must find a way, or the dead will not stay dead."

My mother coughs, then reaches for her lamp. "I'm tired, Nado. I need my sleep."

She slips a finger into the lamp, then her body—smoke, that it is—curls into it, leaving me alone at the table.

"Heal death," I say to myself, eyeing Illyas's pomegranate seed on the shelf. "I need a way into death first." I take the seed off the shelf.

Each seed, a soul of the dead, is a connection to death itself, created from the soil and water and air of death's realm.

I could eat the seed, I think, and then return to the cemetery, but it's no guarantee I'd even get into death. And eating Illyas's seed means he will never be able to visit me in life again.

"No, never," I say, shaking my head. I place the seed back on the shelf and pace my home. "There has to be another way."

18

LAYALA DOESN'T RETURN HOME. THE sun has arced past its highest point in the sky, and she's been gone for hours. Her walks never last for more than an hour or so.

"Saqr," I call, "go find her."

I release the hawk and pull my cloak around my shoulders and hurry outside. I have a feeling I know where Layala is, and I fear I'm right.

The cooling day finds me skirting around the marketplace, not wanting to run into anyone or deal with the boys' fathers again. I know the other men sell dried fruits and meat every morning and the last thing I want is to have one of them waving a meat cleaver in my face.

Instead, I take the long path through the woods, my hood down so I can still see to my sides. I don't want that ghoul or its wolf companion sneaking up on me.

Every few steps I pause, listening for anything following me, but there's nothing except forest sounds.

I let out a long breath and take a deep one in. The air is perfumed with the scent of freshly rained earth, wild mushrooms, forest moss, and tree bark. I breathe in again, wishing I could bottle up the smell and take it into my house. It reminds me of my maman, always with her herbs, always in the woods gathering them.

The town outskirts are nestled up against the forest, a low wall marking the edge between the town and the wild. I pass by the wall, its top barely coming up to my knee, and skirt around the piles of wooden logs left in covered bundles to cure before winter's cold.

The ground is soft, and my boots sink into the mud as I hitch up the path. Dirty water pools under the weight of each step, swirling around my feet. I'm glad I wore my thick-soled boots today and not the soft-leather ones I prefer, noiseless as they are.

The air here smells more like animal and cooking food, oil mixed with herbs mixed with dried meats. It smells like people, and I take a quick breath in, then hurry off onto the walking path that passes through most of the villages and towns in this part of the kingdom. One long road that stretches as far as the king's coffer could allow.

The path is a well-trodden one. Not even weeds dare to grow on it for fear of being crushed underfoot. I follow the path, passing by the hut the shepherdess lives in, with her twelve sheep penned behind it. She has a basket of mushrooms left on her front door and a pile of wildflowers picked fresh from the forest floor.

I wave out to the woman, and she smiles, waving back. Last summer, her son fell ill and she came to me, offering a wool blanket for the winter in exchange for medicine.

"Lovely day," she calls out and I agree.

I hurry off, following the path Saqr took to get to the jinn's house the first time I set him loose. I find it nestled under the cover of a moss-shrouded tree. There is a small wooden chair in front of the house, a pair of leather boots sitting on it.

The door is simple, one latch for a lock, no engravings, not even a name or a house number. I knock once and step back. The door remains closed, so I knock again, then glance in through the window. The house is empty, not even pale embers to show someone was in there earlier.

I circle around to the back of the house, but there's no one behind it. Just a slanted shed with three walls, wood piled under it, and a few rusted horseshoes strewn about.

I glance back through the window and spot a tousled bed, the blankets rumpled, pillow thrown to the floor. In the center of the room, a chair sits scraped back from a low table. I notice a short stack of books taking up one corner of the room and papers strewn about the floor.

"Looking for something?" a voice says behind me.

I startle and turn around, hand to my breast.

"Rami," I say, and notice how bright and angry his eyes are. "Has Layala been here?"

"She's gone."

"So, she's been here. Where did she go?"

His face cracks, and then he's hiding his face behind his hands. His shoulders heave and I find myself reaching out to comfort him.

"Tell me where she is, Rami."

He sniffs and looks up at me, his eyes red-rimmed. "I don't know, but she was upset when she was here. She . . ."

My body seizes, my heart clenched like a tight fist in my chest. "Rami. Tell me now!" I ball my fists and let them drop like stones to my side.

"I don't know! Really! But she said it was her time and that I shouldn't have to die when it was her time. The river . . . she—"

"You should have come to me immediately! You should have stopped her," I say, but I'm already running off. I think I hear him yell, "I'm sorry!" but I don't care what he thinks, how he feels.

No no no no no no no no no no no no no no no no no no no no no no no no no.

It's the only thing running through my mind.

Layala. No no no no no no.

I'm running like a wolf, faster than even Saqr when he dashes out of the house and into the freedom of the sky.

But I don't feel free. I feel shackled and tangled by fear.

Layala. Be well. Be safe. Be sound.

But I'm afraid of what I will find at the river.

Branches slap at me but, in my fear, in my anger, I slap them right back. I want to snap every one of them in half. But I'm barely paying attention to anything, even the thorns that tear through my cloak, as if trying to hold me back from what I may find.

I jump over fallen logs, and not once do I trip, fear making me quick and nimble. Stones and boulders are nothing as I jump over them.

The gurgle of the water reaches me before I see it, and I can smell how cold it is. The soil is soft, and my boots squelch as I speed closer to the river.

And there I find her, face down in the river, her dress snagged on a branch jutting into the water. I can see only part of her back, the rest hidden by the river.

No no no no no no no no no no no.

No no no no no no no.

No!

Not again. No.

Her name tears from my throat, and I stumble into the river, twisting her body around so she can face the sky. But her skin is pale, her lips blue, and I know, I know with all my heart, I know that my child is dead.

"Layala!" I scream.

She doesn't reply.

"Layala!"

I free her dress and pull her water-heavy body to the river's bank. Her skin is cold. Her nails, always so pink, are blue.

I'm flinging myself to the ground and shaking her. But her eyes are closed, and her skin pale, far too pale.

"Layala, hiyati." I pull her on to my lap, rocking her like I always did when she was an infant. "My baby," I sob. "You're my baby." Her body smells musty with river water. Her head flops back on her neck as if only threads are keeping it attached to her body.

I prop her upright against a boulder, her long tangles of hair brushed down her back.

And in the brown of the earth, I see what I don't want to see. Bright red and small. Something her mother should never have to see. Her pomegranate seed. I choke on my breath, my arms losing strength. I can't breathe, I can't move, I can only clutch at my baby's body.

Her seed. Her soul seed.

The seed looks so perfect, ripe for the picking. I don't want to touch it. Touching it would make this real. But I force myself to lean over and pick it up. Plump and red, and full of life. *This isn't real. This isn't real.*

But it is real. I pocket her seed and stare down at my Layl, draped still in my arms. *I have her seed.*

I stop for just a breath to wonder why her soul seed has shown up when so many others haven't fallen on my doorstep in days. Why hers is bright red, when others were browned and rotting. *Because she is young and healthy and only just died, that's why.*

But I don't care about seeds or death or anything else. All I can think is Layala is dead.

My baby is dead. And my heart dies with her.

"Kamuna!" I scream. "Death!"

I lay Layala gently aside and scramble into the river, calling out for Kamuna.

"Kamuna! Come to me!" I shriek and sob.

Birds fly out of the trees, and I hear a wolf howl in the distance.

"Kamuna!"

"I am here."

I spin, water sloshing around me.

"Layala," I say breathlessly. "Lay—"

I heave myself to the river's bank and crawl toward my child.

Kamuna follows and drops to her knees beside me.

"What . . . I—" she begins.

"She's dead," I cry. "She—"

"She drowned."

I swallow back what I'm afraid to say. "Did you have something to do with this?"

"Me?" Kamuna says with a dry laugh. "The girl came here looking for *me*. She wanted to talk. So, I listened."

"What did she want from you?"

"What I offered her before. A chance to live."

My head is pounding, my thoughts swirling. "So, you *drowned* her? After I promised to raise your child?"

"No, Hakawati," she says, her voice cutting sharp into my thoughts. "I did not drown your child. She came to me, and I left her sound and well."

"Then wh-what happened?"

Kamuna looks around, and I notice her squinting at something. "What is that?"

She's already reaching out for a tuft of something gray and white and matted. "Fur?"

My blood runs cold. I look down at Layala, and realize a few stray pieces of short, gray hair are stuck to her skin.

"Wolf," I say.

"There's no blood," Kamuna points out.

"Ghoul."

Her eyebrows shoot up. "A ghoul did this? Well, I can't say I'm surprised. My realm has been sick for a while, souls escaping and roaming as ghouls are bound to happen. But why not take her skin as its own?"

But I'm shaking my head. "It's revenge, I met a ghoul . . ." But I stop myself. It doesn't matter.

"You met a ghoul and then?"

"I need to raise her," I say, ignoring her question.

"She is dead, Hakawati. I told you all borrowed time . . ."

"Rami said—"

"Rami?" Kamuna cuts in, her back stiffening. "What does he have to do with this?"

Did he know? Did he know Layala was going to meet Death? Did he send the ghoul and his wolf after her? I shake my head of the thoughts. *He wouldn't. What would he gain?*

Yet, a small voice inside me whispers, *he would live. He would not take her place.* "Nothing. Nothing. I need to raise her, Death."

"Hakawati," Death begins. "You have her soul seed?"

I nod.

"Then this is her fate. To become Death. I can pass my mantle—"

"No!" I say, and pull Layala closer to my chest. "No."

"Hakawati. She is dead. But you can give her new life."

"She must live," I argue. "In life, not in death."

"Hakawati." Kamuna's lips tighten. "Sayil died, and I could do nothing about it."

"Then you know what I'm feeling now, Kamuna. Give me back Layala; give my child her life back. You did it before."

"You have her soul seed. She is gone, Hakawati. Nothing more to be done—"

"No. No. I am not going to let my child—"

"She is dead."

I shake my head. "No. I can't—"

Kamuna sighs heavily and says, "You will need a sacrifice. How would you even get one? There is no one."

"I know." I glance up at her, her face blank. "Help me. Mother to mother, help me."

"You can't rob death of a soul without touching me," Kamuna says. "Especially a soul that has no story of its own. You didn't make up a story for her, Hakawati, you took part of mine. I *gave* it to you, because as much as it's my job to maintain Death, I hate seeing babies die."

"Help me, Kamuna. Please. As a mother, help me. If not me, then her."

"I cannot. I allowed you once to raise her, and I did so as a mother. I allowed you to. But now . . ." She shrugs. "Now she can take my mantle. So long as I am with my child, I do not care for anything else. If Sayil and I both pass through Mote, I would be happy. If Sayil had taken on my mantle and I remained in death as a soul, I would be happy."

"And what of my happiness?" I cry. "What of my Layala's happiness?"

"You both have had time in life, and with each other. More time than she should have been allotted."

"You are death itself," I say. "You can help—"

"Wait a moment," she interrupts, switching our trail of conversation. "You think Rami knew what she was going to do?"

"He said he didn't know. He only knew she was upset."

Kamuna's face screws up. "Are we so sure a ghoul did this? Any wolf could drink from the river, leave fur behind."

"I don't know what to think. She had fur on her back, on her dress."

"Your mind is muddled with grief, Hakawati. Think for a breath. Rami said he knew she was upset, but then why did he not come to you at once? Why did he not try to stop her or go after her to make sure she was fine?"

"I-I don't know."

"No," Kamuna says, shaking her head. "She did not die by her own hand or even a ghoul's hand. I can feel it. She did not do this."

"He would not have drowned her himself . . ." I begin.

"And why not, Hakawati? He drowned my own child, claimed it was an accident. Perhaps it was, yes, but this," she adds, gesturing at Layala. "This may not have been the ghoul's doing."

I sniff, still hugging Layala's wet, heavy body to my heart.

"If he did this to your child, why is he still alive?" I ask. "Why did you not kill him the moment you knew he killed her?"

Kamuna holds my gaze for a breath. "I have my reasons."

I don't press her, but I stumble to my feet, still carrying Layala's weight in my arms.

"Help me take her home, then," I say.

"I will, but after, I am going to find that jinn. Because I don't, for a moment, believe some ghoul did this."

I'm still crying, my face wet with tears and river water. "She didn't think it was fair, that her time had come yet she would not have to die for it. She did not think it fair that Rami should die when—"

"If she had those thoughts, I have no doubt Rami would have preyed upon them. Even encouraged them, Hakawati. He wormed himself into my daughter's mind, once. She loved him, as a young girl loves any boy, and she vowed to always be with him. I knew this, I saw them steal secrets with each other, and I was stupid to not have stopped them when I should have. But I thought, they are young, they are stupid, but they will learn."

I stare at Death for a moment. My thoughts flit back to when I knew Layala was with a boy, when I told myself to let her be, that she would come to me when she was ready.

"Why not tell me this before?" I want to slam my fist into her throat, but my hands are weighted with Layala's body. *My baby's body.*

"I should have. I was too concerned with my own business. I am sorry, Hakawati."

I nod, not quite accepting her apology, but not dismissing it, either. "If you're right, Death, I will slay him myself."

"If I'm right, I will be right beside you. And if I'm not, then she has made her choice, Hakawati. Or the ghoul has made it for her."

19

We carry Layala back to our home and lay her down in her cot. The first thing I do is place her seed in the same glass jar as her father's, in the holding waters from the river of death.

"I will raise you, my Layala," I tell her as she lies dead in her cot.

Kamuna has already left to find Rami.

"No matter by whose hand it is you drowned, I will raise you."

I stare down at her body and think how small she looks, when just a few days ago she looked so long-limbed to me.

"I will find a sacrifice, Layl. Don't you worry, your maman will find you a sacrifice."

I glance at Illyas's soul seed, nestled in the jar of river water.

"No, never," I say. "I will never sacrifice him."

But I keep glancing at the jar, with the crimson seed so bright and red, so perfectly preserved.

I shake my head and get to work.

I wash her body as gently as if she were a newborn. With warm cloths and rose-scented salt to scrub the sweat and river water off her skin, I wash my daughter's body as if she's still a babe fast asleep.

Her skin is soft and has a smoothness and tautness to it I haven't noticed recently. Her limbs are lithe, muscled even, and as I clean her long, lean legs, I notice how shapely they are, how *strong*. Her whole body is coiled tightness, young and healthy.

"I will bring you back, hiyati," I tell Layala. "I will not let you stay dead."

I cry until I'm done washing her, until I've cleaned all the dirt staining her skin, until I've dried and dressed her and she's tucked in bed. I perch beside her on the cot, rubbing her face with oils to keep it from drying out. I brush her hair, braid it, and sit down to tell her a story. It's one I told her when she was a child, when she was cranky and refused to go to bed.

And so, I tell her the story now, choking out words in between the sobs, trying to control my voice as if she could hear me.

A princess once lived among peas and carrots, squash and zucchini, eggplant and yams. She was poor, even though she was a princess. But she lived happy in her gardens, growing what she needed to eat and selling the little left over in the village market.

One season, the harvest was poor, and the princess had little to eat. She cried to herself about starving during the winter, but resolved to make do. She would live, even if she went to bed hungry every night.

So, she gathered up her little crop, stored them away in jars and clay pots, and settled herself in for the winter.

The winter that year was cruel. The wind gust up in howling rages, leaving snow in its wake every night, blocking the front of her door. The princess didn't know what she could do; she had firewood to keep her warm, but only a gardener's shovel to remove the snow. But the shovel she used, doing all she could every day and settling in by her fire at night.

One evening, as she was making her meager stew of one potato, one carrot, and a few beans, someone knocked on her door.

"Who could that be?" asked the princess, setting down her stirring spoon and wiping her hands on her apron. She covered the distance from her fire to the door in five paces, so small was the hut she lived in, and she opened the door. But when she peered out, no one was there.

Shivering against the cold and the snow, the princess shut the door and went back to her fire. But soon after, she heard the knocking again.

"Who could that be?" repeated the princess as she once again opened the door. Again, no one was there. She returned to her fire and stirred her stew.

She heard the knock a third time, and a third time she opened the door. Again, no one was there.

This time, the princess grew annoyed, and she slammed the door shut and turned around to her fire. There, an old man stood, hunched over her stew.

"Come," he told her. "Sit. I will pour you a bowl of this delicious-smelling stew you have here."

The princess, frightened, obeyed the man, though she eyed the shovel near the door.

"May I share of your meal?" the old man asked.

The princess, too frightened to speak, could only nod, and watched as the man poured himself a small bowl, before handing another to her. She took it with shaking hands and set it down at the table, not trusting herself to eat.

"Who are you?" she finally asked.

The man only smiled as he blew on his spoon and slurped the stew.

"Tell me who you are," the princess said, strength entering her voice. Anger was replacing her fear.

"I am a mage," the man said, "come to give you a better life."

"I am happy here," the princess said.

"You are a princess and could have so much more, yet you live here, alone, with barely anything to eat, and only a bit of wood to keep the cold from seeping into your bones."

"But I am happy. There is no place I would rather be than here."

"Perhaps that is because you know of no other place, little *amira*," the mage said. *Little princess*.

"I know enough to know this is my home. I am happy here."

"Very well," the mage said, and loosened something from around his neck. "Take this chain and sleep with it under your pillow for a fortnight. I will return. If you wish to remain here then, I will leave you be."

The princess took the chain with a large stone attached to it and dangled it before her. "What is it?" she asked.

"It will show you worlds beyond your own. Cities, people, dreams you've never dared to dream." He held up his hand when the princess opened her mouth to ask more questions. "I will return in a fortnight. You may ask your questions then."

And so the mage left the princess, the chain still dangling in her hand.

That night, the princess slept with the stone under her pillow, and that night she dreamt of a town she'd never even heard of before. The town was three, four, five, six times larger than her own. It boasted houses and buildings steepled in blues and golds, greens, purples. The townspeople were just as fine, with their brightly colored clothes, their decadent furs, their faces painted with rouge and kohl.

When the princess awoke, she found herself longing for that town. "It was just a dream," she told herself, but she found herself impatient for the night to come, even though it was still morning and she'd only just woken.

The day passed slowly for her, and as soon as night came, the princess threw herself into her bed and closed her eyes to sleep.

This night's dream told of a land far, far away from hers, where horses were used to pull carriages through a city, rather than in the farms. The people in this dream were finer than those in the last, and they wore brighter colors with intricate cuts of their clothes. They wore jewels and gold, silver and more. And they sparkled in all their splendor.

The morning left the princess aching for that land, to visit it, to see it, to smell it, and most of all, to wear what those people wore.

She waited for nightfall and soon found herself once more, asleep. That night, she dreamt of another land, this one filled with handsome princes and fine castles. The princess saw herself watching the castles from afar, and even in her dream, her longing to enter the castles grew to an ache. She awoke upset and flustered and tore the necklace from under her pillow. She threw it into the fire, cursing at it for making her unhappy with her life, for now her little hut seemed small and ugly in comparison to the lands she was seeing in her dreams.

But that night, the princess found herself pulling the stone out of the fire and cooling it before laying it back under her pillow. And again, that night, she dreamt of lands far, far away, with colors brighter than she'd ever seen and people more beautiful than she could imagine.

And so, the fortnight passed.

On the appointed night, the mage returned.

"So, little amira, what do you think? Shall I whisk you off to lands far, far away? Or shall I leave you here, content in your little hut and garden?"

The princess hesitated, for though she loved her home and the people she knew, the lands in her dreams called to her and an ache gnawed in her belly.

"Take me to them," the princess finally said. "I want to see more of this life."

The mage smiled and held his hand out for the necklace. The princess gave it to him, and he clasped it back around his neck.

"A life not lived in splendor is not a life lived," the mage said, now offering his hand to her. "And I will give you splendor, and more, little amira."

The princess reached out her hand to the mage, but pulled it back right before their fingers touched. "Why me?" she asked. "And why now?"

"Your time has come, little amira. Your family has called for you to return to them."

"My family?"

The mage nodded. "Your family which has been kept away from you; they have called for your return."

"My family," the princess mused. "I didn't know I had any."

"Ah, but you do, little amira. An old wicked witch kept you from them, but your family called upon me to bring you back to them. But they only want you back if you want to be with them."

"The places in my dreams, they are where my family are?"

The mage nodded. "You will have riches and splendor, castles and balls, gowns and jewels, and so much more. You will have your birthright, little amira. That and so much more."

When I'm done telling her the story, I make sure she's tucked in tight and lean over to kiss her cheek. She smells of honey and oils, but there's something missing, something of her own scent that isn't there.

I choke back a sob and turn to the jar with her seed in it. I will eat the dirt of a grave, drink the water of the river of death, and even drain my blood, if that's what it takes to bring my baby back.

But first, I need a sacrifice.

20

"HE'S NOT HERE PRESENTLY," THE manservant says, but I push past him. My shoulder bumps into his and he coils away, as if struck by a snake.

"I'll wait for him then," I say as I make my way down the hall to the sheikh's study. I knock once and hear a gruff voice telling me to come in.

"Not home?" I snap, shooting the manservant a look as I open the study's door. The manservant glares at me.

Abu Illyas's face turns sour when he recognizes me. "You," he says.

"Yes, me." I don't wait for him to offer me a chair. I take the one before his desk and sit, staring at him. He's hunched in his chair, his hands folded on the desk. But he's staring at me with those cold snake eyes. I hold his gaze evenly.

"What do you want?"

"Layala is dead. She drowned in the river."

I give him a moment to let the thought sink in. And just as he opens his mouth—no doubt to blame me—I interrupt.

"I need a sacrifice."

He knows what I mean.

I notice Sheikh Hamadi's throat rise and fall as he swallows. "A sacrifice. I won't do it, jinn. You should have—"

"You have one day to decide. You and I are the last ones alive who care for her, who could be a sacrifice."

"Then why don't you die for her?" He points a finger at me. "She is *your* child."

"And *your grand*child. If I were to be the sacrifice, then who would raise her? No," I shake my head, "you need me alive to do the raising."

"I will never die for you, jinn!" Abu Illyas shouts, jumping to his feet. "For you, *never!*"

My voice is cool and even. "It's not for me, it's for Layl."

He blinks in surprise, as if only now considering what I am truly asking, what this means for Layala.

"Your sacrifice would bring Layala back."

"And if you fail to bring her back?"

"I wouldn't."

He clears his throat and stares down his nose at me. "How could she drown? Where were you to prevent this?"

I don't reply.

"You should die, jinn, for all the trouble you've caused me. I should drown you myself."

You think I don't want to die, now that my child is dead, you old fool? But if I'm dead, she will remain dead.

"I would die for her, but it would be too much—"

"Too much for who, jinn?" the sheikh says with a sneer. "You *should* die for your child, for the danger you've put her in. It's because of you," he says, pointing a sharp finger at me, "because of you she is now dead."

"I will bring her back," I insist. "With your sacrifice."

"You've struck whatever deal with Death or with the devil or whomever to even be able to have your dealings with death. But I'll have no part in it." He waves the air in front of his face, as if clearing it of his words. "*You* die to bring Layl back, and I will take her in. She'll be where she belongs."

"You don't understand, old man," I say, my temper rising. "Layala is *dead.*"

"Get out, jinn."

"Layala is dead because—"

"I said, get out!"

I'm slamming my fist against his desk before I realize what I'm doing. The old man jumps, startled, and I force my voice to sound even, calm.

"I can bring Layala back. But there is only one way to do this. A willing sacrifice." My words are slow, clear. He *has to* understand.

Abu Illyas eyes me sharply, then slumps back into his seat. "There is . . . no . . . other way?"

He studies me through his bushy brows, his thin lips pursed tight enough they're a white slit across his face.

I shake my head.

His body stiffens, even as his face falls.

Finally, he says, "And if I . . . die? If I die, she *will* be safe? She will be cared for? How?"

"Just as she always has been—by her mother."

His cheeks flush red in anger. "You were never a mother, jinn. She died before, and now again, under your eye, under *your* care. I should have imprisoned—"

"Should have, would have, it doesn't matter. We're both here now, and Layala is lying dead in her cot."

Abu Illyas says nothing for several breaths, his face draining of color with each exhale. "I have lived many years, many of them alone. I have no one left but Layala to care for." His chin quivers for a moment, but then he clenches his jaw and steels it once more. "I will do it, jinn. For Layala, not for you."

"I know it's for Layl."

The sheikh turns his back to me as he says, "Leave me be. Come back in the morning. I will have all my papers organized. The estate, inheritance, everything, I leave for Layala. She will want for nothing. She will live here and be cared for by the servants."

"Shukran," I say, my voice catching. "I . . . Layala—" I take a deep breath and continue. "She may never forgive me for sacrificing you," I say.

He understands my meaning. "I will write her a note and tell her I would sacrifice my last breath, my last drop of blood, for her, over and over again."

I nod, my chin and jaw aching trying not to cry. "Shukran, Abu Illyas. Sheikh Hamadi."

"You're not welcome. Now leave."

21

I STUMBLE BACK TO MY house. My baby is still in her cot, though I half-hoped I would find her puttering about the house, making a pot of tea and telling me, "Maman, look, it was just a bit of water."

But my daughter is still dead, and I still hold her soul seed. This is not a nightmare I can wake up from.

I wonder, for just a single, mournful breath, *What would her soul's story be?*

But that is not something I ever want to know, because it would mean she is dead, fully dead, and could never be raised again.

I don't have the energy to try visiting death, to find Illyas and tell him. I'm not sure I could even get into death regardless, not with Kamuna's death seed rotting. Instead, I rub my daughter's limbs with more oil, tuck the blankets around her, and lie down beside her, wrapping my arms around her still body. I am asleep before I've taken several breaths.

The morning wakes me with heavy knocks on my door.

I slip out of bed, not wanting to move away from Layala, but also wanting to open the banging door, if only to make the noise stop.

"Coming, coming," I say over the riot of a pounding fist.

I open the door, half-expecting to see Abu Illyas standing before me. But it's not him, or his servant, or anyone from his house.

It's three of the town's guards, with faces set as grim as tombstones.

"We are here to arrest you on charges of—"

"Arrest me? What, no!" I say, but the guard continues as if I've said nothing.

"—on charges of murder, attempted murder, and deceit of a high-ranking townsman. You will appear in court in two days' time, where you will be tried before—"

"Sheikh Hamadi sent you, didn't he?" I interrupt.

The guard says nothing, but the two behind him move forward to grab me.

"I don't have time for this," I say, putting my hands out to stop them. They freeze, just like the ghoul's wolf did, and before either of them can blink, they're clay figurines.

The first guard opens his mouth and closes it like a fish stolen from the sea.

"You next," I say, and turn him into clay. The last of my energy used, I slump forward, stumbling before righting myself.

I pick up all three and, though I want to smash them to pieces, I set them onto the table. I'm tired, my bones feeling too heavy to carry. And I think, *I should not have done this. I as good as killed them; I cannot raise them from clay. Cannot bring them back. Animals can be brought back, but humans, humans have a soul that cannot be threaded so easily back into bone and blood.*

Guilt settles like a rock in my stomach. *I defended myself and my child, and not a drop of blood spilled. I did what any mother would have done.*

I turn to my child, her face so pale, her limbs too stiff, lips far too blue. "Well, Layl," I say, "it seems your jido has broken his promise."

With no other options, I shut the door, still talking to Layala as if she can hear me. "I will find a willing sacrifice. But first, I must speak to your grandfather." I gather the clay guards, throw them into a pack, and with a piece of bread in my hand to keep my strength up, I leave the house and Layl behind, making sure the door is locked, checking it once, then twice.

Then I make my way to Sheikh Hamadi's house, the clay figurines clinking in my pack.

As I draw closer to town, I shield my face with the hood of my cloak. No doubt Sheikh Hamadi has alerted half the town already on my supposed attempted murder.

"The idiot," I say to myself. "Does he think he can raise Layala on his own, without her mother?"

I get to his house, but I don't step up to the front gates. I take the back, the servants' corridor, and sneak in the way Illyas and I used to sneak out when we were younger.

The servants don't take notice of me, busy as they are prepping what looks to be a large meal.

I slip by, clinging to walls and keeping my head down.

Once inside the main section of the house, I sneak down the halls and make my way to the east wing. There's a room there, filled with family heirlooms, daggers and old swords. I take a few, tucking one under my cloak, another at my hip, and slip a dagger into my boot.

The room has a second door, a hidden one, noticeable only if you know where to look. I press on the wall, and part of it creaks open.

A musty draft hits me, and it smells faintly of cooking oils and herbs coming from the kitchen and the old stone and earth of the house itself.

I shut the door behind me and follow the tunnel to Sheikh Hamadi's study.

There are raised voices when I get there, the sheikh's and another man's. I cock my head to the side to hear better. No, *two* other men, at least. I press my ear to the wall, trying to hear through the stone.

"She has never caused us trouble," one of the men say.

"She is a jinn, and all jinns are trouble!" Sheikh Hamadi says. "She murdered my granddaughter—"

"Are you sure she did it? Why would she come to you if she did?"

"I told you, she wanted me to come to the house. She wants to kill me. She was trying to lure me—"

"Why didn't you call the town guards immediately? Why wait until this morning?"

"I-I was making sure my affairs were in order, if anything were to happen."

"And where is the girl, then? Why didn't you send guards to get the girl?"

"I . . . Layala . . . I . . ."

It was the first time I'd heard Sheikh Hamadi blubber. I let myself enjoy it for a moment before turning my attention back to what the men are saying.

"Where is the girl, Sheikh?"

"At the jinn's lair, no doubt. Or in a grave."

"We've already sent three men to get the jinn," the third man says. "They were ordered to retrieve the girl as well and bring her here."

"I want that jinn dead," Sheikh Hamadi says. "Like the rest of her kind should be."

"Once the girl is safe—"

"The jinn said she's dead!" he interrupted.

"Again, why wait until morning to send guards?"

I hold my breath, waiting for an answer.

"I assumed the jinn was lying about her death. I thought Layala would see through the jinn's doing and come to me. It would have been easier to claim custody of her, like I should have years ago when my son died at that jinn's hands!" A fist slams on a table and I assume it's Abu Illyas's.

"With respect, Sheikh, but did Illyas, did he not die for his child? My own father, before he died, told me—"

"That girl would never have died in the first place if that jinn—"

"You just said you assumed she wasn't dead, Sheikh," the second man says.

"I should have said I *hoped* she wasn't dead," Abu Illyas starts.

The first man interrupts. "That jinn told my father's story. I still remember it. I went to her, three days after we buried him. And she told me she captured the story, because she knew him. She wrote down his story. I still have it."

"That jinn deceives and betrays," Sheikh Hamadi says. "She took my son from me, she seduced him and forced him to stay with her once her child was born. And then she seduced him again, convincing him to kill himself."

The man lowers his voice. "With all respect, Sheikh, they were young."

I don't catch what Sheikh Hamadi says, but I catch the mood in his voice.

"I want her dead!" I hear finally. "Dead and burned so she could never be raised!"

"I cannot order the killing of Nadine—of the Hakawati, without proof of ill doing," the man says.

"I agree," the second man says. "We have a law to uphold, and we do so with justice."

"Ach," Sheikh Hamadi says, and I hear things being flung across the room. "Your law is worthless to me!"

"Then why call for us and our guards before the sun has barely opened its eyes? You were keen on sending guards to arrest the Hakawati."

"I thought you fools would do something!"

"We are. We are upholding our law."

"Damn you and your law. I'll do it myself."

A few moments later, the stone wall of the tunnel shakes as a door slams.

The men say something to each other, and then I hear the door shut again, gentler this time.

I creep back to the weapons room, but as I'm opening the door, I spot movement inside.

It's the sheikh. I'm not the only one who decided to arm themselves with the family weapons. When he leaves the room, I pad out of the tunnel, opening the door just enough to look through a crack before barreling back through the servants' way.

"Ay, you!" a servant says, "with the cloak. Where are you going? Get back in the kitchens!"

"*Hadayr,*" I say. *Yes, of course.*

They don't wait to see if I obey; they're too busy scurrying around. Once outside, I run as if wolves are at my heels. Run back to my house, the sheikh's weapons clinking against me.

He's coming to kill me, and though I want to wring his scrawny little neck and be done with him, I know I shouldn't.

I shouldn't because I need him to sacrifice himself for Layala. And that's what I'll get him to do.

22

I'M ALREADY HOME TENDING THE fire when fists pound on my door again. Saqr hasn't returned yet, either, and I'm wondering where he is.

I stifle a sigh and with a glance at Layala, I move to open the door. It's Sheikh Hamadi.

"Move, move, jinn," he says and pushes me out of my own doorway. Barging toward Layala, I can see his knees buckle, but he catches himself and kneels beside her.

"Laylaloon," he sobs, taking her hand in his. "My little kushtbani."

My anger with him melts just a bit seeing him so soft with Layala.

"You killed her," he says, his voice gravelly, not looking up at me.

"She drowned," I say, and the compassion I was just feeling for him hardens back into steel.

"You should have been with her! You should have done something, jinn!"

He's on his feet now, barreling toward me. I grab a clay figurine and hold it before me. "One step closer and you'll end up like those guards you sent after me."

He freezes, eyeing the figurine. "I was wondering where those bastards got to," he said. "But I'll finish what they couldn't." He slaps the figurine out of my hand, and it shatters against the hard floor. "He's dead now," I say. "You killed him. I can't put broken clay pieces back together and bring them to life."

He ignores my words and moves to grab my arm, but I sidestep him and kick him in the back of the knee. I slip my hand around his shoulder and latch his neck in the crook of my elbow.

He's on his knees, caught in my grip. And though he's strong, he's still an old, grieving man.

"You want Layala alive?" I ask.

"Y-yes," he chokes.

"So do I," I say, tightening my grip on him. He struggles, but he's too weak against me. "I want you to die," I say. "I want you to die so Layala can live."

He gasps something, but I don't catch his words.

"You have to agree to sacrifice yourself," I say. "An angry or vengeful soul is no good to me. You have to sacrifice yourself and leave in love for her to be raised."

"I-I will kill you, jinn," he sputters.

"Give yourself," I say. "For Layala." I try to make my voice soft and soothing, to calm him.

His skin is turning paler than ever.

"Sacrifice yourself," I say.

"For Lay-for Lay-Layala," he wheezes.

"Yes, for Layala. Do you?"

"Y-y- . . ." Then he grunts and I know he's agreed. His body slackens against mine.

But is he willing enough? Will this work? Did I make a mistake, forcing his hand like this?

I shove those thoughts out of my mind. *This* has *to work.* I loosen my grip on him, letting him catch his breath.

"I will be merciful," I say. "And I will tell your soul's story."

His eyes are bright and wet as he glances back at me. "Te-tell her I l-l-love her. And Illyas. Tell him-tell him I love him . . ."

I soften my voice more. "I will do that."

"I . . . tell Layala I-I would have done it again and again for her. She is worth more to me than the blood in my veins and the soul in my body."

"I will make sure she knows, but I know she already does."

The sheikh hangs his head, then raises it, looking ahead. I'm still behind him, waiting for him to release whatever anger is left in him, to accept his death and sacrifice.

"Do it, jinn," he says, his voice gruff. "But always remember this, I do it for Layala, never for you."

"I know."

He nods once, then lifts his head so his chin is high in the air.

"For Layala," he says. I grab his neck from behind and slide his family dagger across his throat.

I let Abu Illyas's body drop to the ground and lay him flat before I drag him closer to the fire. Beside him is his soul seed. It's in my hand before I know what I'm doing, and I place it on the shelf beside his son's pomegranate seed. "Shukran, for your sacrifice," I say. "It won't be in vain."

23

I know I need to tell Illyas. And I need to find Layala's soul in death.

I'll try once more to get into death. Marrow and mud might get me in.

I raise my eyes to the heavens and pray, pray I will be able to enter death this day.

I have a few ghoul bones stored in jars, and I slip them into my pocket as I make my way to the cemetery. There, I chew on the bones, sucking the marrow out as quickly as I could, chanting and praying all the while. I drink from my canteen, filled with water from death's river. And I eat the bones themselves, wincing as they slice down my throat to my stomach.

Let me in, death. Let me in. Let me in. Let me in.

I chant, and drink, and eat, and swallow grave dirt and stone and marrow and bone.

Just as I am about to give up, a tingle shoots through my body. I feel as if I'm underwater, drowning.

And as I'm gasping, I feel that familiar lighting strike through my body, and I enter the grayness and stillness of death.

Paths swerve ahead of me, each one going in a different direction, giving the illusion of choice. Birds the size of my fist flutter in the green-purple sky, clumps of feathers missing from their small bodies. A small fox, more a pale pink than the fiery orange of life, sits and watches me before turning his tail in my direction and sauntering away.

"Layala!" I choke as I stumble forward.

Death smells like rot, and I gag, dry heaving as I fall to my knees. I ignore the roiling nausea and force myself to stand. Swaying on my feet, my hands reaching out to grab something, anything, to not stumble and vomit all over. My knees almost buckle, but I catch myself and settle back into my stride.

"Illyas!" I cry. "Where are you?"

I hurry off, through death's Waiting Place, through the stillness that weighs heavily around me.

"Illyas?" I call.

The Waiting Place, which should be filled with souls waiting to pass into Mote, is empty. The land is a small area, mostly made of watered-down colors, a pale imitation of life. Patches of grass more gray than green dot the ground, bending in a breeze I cannot feel. Flowers, white and gray and black and shades in between stand idly, as if waiting for permission to wilt and die.

The stones are cracked, the gaps wide enough I can fit my fist into them. And what used to be green is yellow now, yellow and brown and the color of rust. Even pieces of the sky are missing, leaving black spaces behind, like shards of glass.

Death is decaying. Death is decaying. Death is decaying.

I shove the thoughts away.

"Layl?" I call out, taking the handle of the single white door floating in a mist of clouds and water droplets.

The door opens and lets me through, revealing a town beyond. The streets are a pale blue, washed out gray cobblestone, with rows of pale gray light torches lining it. Small stone cottages sit connected to each other on either side of the streets, dull white light flooding out from the candles lit at their windows. The sky above me is a washed out purple, with clouds that look sickly in their off-whiteness and their shriveled, floating appearance.

"Layl? Illyas?" I call out, glancing into each window I pass.

Souls, like bodies, lay in beds or sprawled out on the cottage floors. A few sit in chairs, turning the pages of blank books, as if staring at the pages would make words appear.

"Layl!" I yell louder. "It's maman!"

A bird the size of my palm darts before me, startling me back a step. It rests atop one of the tall torches, cocking its head as it follows my movements.

"Nado?" I hear a voice say. Then, "Maman!"

Two shadowy figures approach, and I run to them, stumbling over my own feet.

"Layala!" I cry, taking her into my arms, only for her to turn to smoke and reappear before me.

"Maman?" she says. "Why—"

"It's death, baby, you have no body."

I turn to look at Illyas, who's frowning. "Nado," he says. "Where have you been? I couldn't visit you."

"I couldn't get in; death wouldn't let me. But first," I say, turning back to Layala. "Tell me, Layl. What happened at the river?"

But her lips curl up into a tight line, and she says nothing.

"Layl. You have to tell me."

"I fell in, I think," she says, but she's not looking me in the eye. And her arms are crossed tight over her chest. "But I remember feeling a hand on my back."

"Oh, Layl," I say and want to squeeze her so tight.

"Maman, really, I drowned. It happens. I'm . . . happy. I can now take on Death's mantle, I can have a purpose."

"No, Layl, it doesn't just happen. Tell me who pushed you. Tell me, because your jido sacrificed himself for you."

Illyas goes still. "Nado?" he questions softly.

"I'm sorry, Illyas. Truly, I am."

Layala screams.

"I *died*, maman. I died. I am meant to die!"

She's on her knees now, hunching into herself. I want to take her into my arms, soothe her. But I can't.

"Please, Layl, you have to tell me."

"You!" she shouts and moves away from me. "You did this to him."

"I have to raise you, Layl. And the only way—"

"No, you don't. You should leave me dead. I was ready to die, maman. I didn't want to, but then I did. And I'm—"

"No, no, Layl, no. You can't die, not now," I argue. "That can't be. I found you. You should have been floating down the river or at its bottom. You can't say you were meant to die if it wasn't a natural death."

"I don't know, maman. I remember something pushing me in, then something else pulling me out, but I was fading." She's screwing up her face, and I know death makes it difficult to remember things, especially for a young soul.

She must note my strain, because she smiles softly. "It's okay, maman. I should have been dead all these years. And Rami should not die. Sayil should not have to take Death's mantle, not if I am willing."

"But you're not, Layl. You can't."

"Yes, maman, I am, and I will."

"No, no, Layl, please," I say, and I'm on my knees begging my own child to let me bring her back to life.

She kneels before me, and her voice is hushed now. "I'm sorry, maman, but I'm dead. I'm here, and I'm dead, and I'm with baba. And I'll find jido."

"I'll be alone," I say. "And you, you were to have a long, happy life."

"I will, maman!" she says, laughing now. "Don't you see? I will have a *reason* for my life. I will be Death."

"You can't stay dead, Layl. I can't—I won't accept that."

My fingers itch to touch her, to pull her in to me. But I keep them at my side. "Listen, Layl, I am your mother, and nothing is more important to me than you. Nothing. Not my life, not even your father's, nothing."

Her face contorts and her shoulders shake, but in death there are no tears. My heart twists and I want to pull her out of death and sit her by the fire in our home and tell her that everything will be fine.

I get to my feet now, and I stare at Layl. "I am bringing you back to life, Layala. And so help me, you are going to stay alive this time."

She looks at me with those wide, wide eyes. "Maman, no. I will drown myself again and again if I have to."

"Layala," Illyas says. "Your mother is right. She is giving you another chance—"

"Don't you see?" Layala shrieks. "I want this. I want to be Death. I want the mantle passed to me. I want to do *something* with my life. And this is it!"

"No!" Illyas and I yell at the same time.

Layala takes a step back, and before Illyas can reach out for her, she's running. Running away from us, her back the last I see of her before she disappears behind a cloud of mist.

Illyas turns to me, his eyes mournful. "Bring her back, Hakawati. If it's the last thing you do."

24

My hands know what to do before my mind does. Trailing her skin, I pour warm oil over it and rub herbs into the creases at her elbows, knees, and neck.

Her body lies before the fire, kept warm by the crackling flames. I tie her oiled hair in a braid as thick as my fist and wrap it around her head like a crown. The oil gives the strands a sheen, a mimicry of what it was in life. But no matter, her hair will soon be shiny and vibrant with life again.

Abu Illyas's body is beside her. The back of his head, covered with hair white and thick, is a muddled purple color from the pooled blood. His back and shoulders are also a mottled purple and brown, but that makes it easier for me to insert a needle into his flesh and let out the blood I'll need.

The worst part is letting my own blood. To do a proper raising, there has to be fresh blood for the body being raised.

I turn Abu Illyas's body over and insert the needle into his back. The blood is dark and thick, and it drains into a bowl through a glass vial the needle is attached to.

I prepare the herbs—mixes of ones so old they're dust, but still potent. Herbs fresh from the woods beyond the cabin, dirt taken from the old cemetery behind my home. Water from the well, mud and clay kneaded together as if I'm baking bread. Heat from the fire and steam from a kettle boiling over it, ash from wood just burned. Marrow from animal bones, salt to sprinkle in.

The bodies were all made of Earth, which gave flesh and bone. The bodies were given souls made of Sky. Blood was brought to life by Fire and Sea.

And so, Death asked her friends, creatures of stone and sand and clay, water and foam and flame, breath and dirt. She asked them for their help.

Earth fashioned a being made of clay and sand and made golems.

Sea made a creature of salt and water and made marids.

Sky took air and cloud wisps and rain and made ghouls.

Fire took ash and smoke and made jinns.

I coat Layala's body first with ash, marring her clean skin with dark smudges. Then I layer her with the mud and clay, a thick coat that would have stiffened her joints if they weren't already stiff.

The herbs and dirt I mix in with the water. Her mouth, shut in death, I have to pry open with a silver spoon. I pour the liquid down her throat, knowing it will only settle in her stomach. The marrow I then mix with the salt and coat her mouth in it. I bring the kettle to her face, a mimicry of breath and air, and let the steam coat her skin, her mouth, settle around her nose.

The sun fades in through the window, and the moon takes over in the sky. And then the moon skips across the sky, until the sun retakes its place, and still I work.

I reach up for the shelf and take Abu Illyas's soul seed down. I lay it gently in a flat dish beside Layala's hand.

That seed I will eat, and I will learn Abu Illyas's soul's story. And it is that story I will weave into Layala's soul, to become part of her.

I bleed myself.

I lean against the foot of the table, facing Layl, and watch as bright red blood flows out my arm through a glass needle. My blood fills a bowl as deep as my wrist, and then I take another bowl to fill.

The lightheadedness comes in waves. My vision blurs. I see spots, and then nothing. I know if I try to stand, I will stumble, so I stay sitting and hang my head down between my knees, the urge to vomit overwhelming me.

Sweat pours down my face, and my body flashes between feeling hot and cold, numb and tingly.

And still, I bleed myself. The second bowl fills up and I take another one, placing the needle's other end into it.

My blood is coming out slower now, my body fighting to keep it in my veins.

A moan escapes from my lips. I am on my hands and knees now, though I want to lie down and go to sleep.

I reach out for Abu Illyas's soul seed, feeling for it with my fingers.

It's a bit cool to the touch, rubbery-skinned. I pop it into my mouth and bite down. The tartness floods my tongue and I chew until my teeth grind the seed into pieces, then I swallow.

The stories flood me. I clutch at one, only to find it tugged out my grasp. My mind can't keep them straight. There are flashes of steel and metal, of wood and ash, of greens and greys and browns and whites.

I see brushstrokes of blood. Smears of ash on skin.

The stories are a jumbled mess that make no sense. I feel pain, a pain so deep I think I will either be consumed by it or grow so numb, that I am nothing but an abyss. My heart aches the way it never has before, aches more than seeing Layala dead, more than when Illyas died. More than when my family was imprisoned. Aches more than all the pain I have ever felt added together.

And the pain gnaws at me. Every thought is threaded through with that pain. My body feels on fire, feels burned and bled and raw and beaten. My soul itself feels as if it's being buried and buried and buried again under fire and steam and heat and ash.

And that could only mean one thing—his soul is in Jahannam. His soul seed is unusable.

I remember something my maman told me once, when I was young. *Your soul seed carries all your good and all your bad within it. Enough wrongdoings, and your seed will end up in Jahannam, unable to pass onto Mote. So be good, child, do good, and keep the bad few and far in between.*

I gasp, ripping the needle out of my arm. Crawling to Abu Illyas, I check on the bowls filled with his blood. The blood is dark and too thick to do much with.

But that doesn't even matter—his soul is unusable. His death was for nothing. And there is no other sacrifice to raise Layala with.

I would have died right then for her if I could have, but there would be no one to raise her, or—to bury her.

My vision is still blurry, and I can't stand without stumbling into the table and chairs. But still I crawl to the door and fling it open.

The cool air is fresh against my skin, and I gulp it in by the mouthful. A crow caws overhead, and I turn my head to it, though I can't see it through my blurry vision. My breath is coming out in spurts, and I hear myself wheezing.

I clutch at my neck, feeling like I'm choking. My child is dead. Layala is dead, and there isn't anything I could do.

I could die, and it would be for nothing. All her family are dead. And my family, imprisoned in metal, would be worthless for a raising.

"Layala!" I scream. The crow startles and I hear it flap its wings hard, shrieking as it flies off.

My mind whirs, and as it whirs, my vision comes back in pieces.

I stand now, though my legs still feel weak, and I slump against the door, then stumble into the table, the chair, until I half-crawl to the fire.

I set the kettle back to boil and throw in leaves that will give me strength. I cut off a heel of bread and shove it into my mouth, not bothering to clean up the crumbs.

And I kiss her face, not caring that mud and clay and ash catch onto my lips. "I'll find a way, Layl," I tell my daughter, still lying dead beside the dying fire. "Even if I have to die for it."

25

I AM HUGGING ILLYAS'S JAR with his seed in it when I hear the knock later that evening.

"I've come to pay my respects," Rami says. I should be surprised to find him standing here. But I am not. I feel nothing but my grief for Layala.

I step aside and let him into the cottage, shutting the door behind me. He pads over to Layala, head bowed.

"What will you do now?" he asks. "Kamuna won't raise my family now that she has Layala."

"I don't care about your family!" I shout. "My child is dead, and you're coming to me with worries about your family?"

I wish I could eat back my words as soon as they are out of my mouth. Rami stands there, his hands hanging limply at his sides.

"I'm sorry, truly," he says. "We've both lost much."

I don't say anything as I sit down, still clutching Illyas's jar.

"I also came to speak with you, Hakawati," Rami says hesitantly. He pulls a chair across from me and sits. "I think you and I can help each other." He glances at the sheikh's body but says nothing about it.

"How so, Rami?"

"Listen, Hakawati, for one moment. You agreed to raise Sayil to take on the mantle, no?"

I nod.

"Well, now that Layala is dead, Kamuna has no reason to wait any longer. She will make Layala Death."

"But then she won't have me to pass Sayil into Mote."

"Eh," Rami says. "You may be the only Hakawati on this side of the sea, but there are others, few; I can count them on one hand, but I am sure she could convince one of them to pass Sayil along. Some favor for a favor."

I sniff, then say, "What are you proposing, then?"

"I know Sayil, from a long time ago. We were close friends, and I know she would want me to be happy. Now, Kamuna I don't trust to fulfill her promises. But Sayil, Sayil I do trust. We can retrieve her body and soul seed from where Death keeps her preserved. And you can raise Sayil before Kamuna has a chance to make Layala Death."

I hesitate, and before I can reply, he says, "Why do you think she hasn't come back to kill me yet? She gave me one day. Well, that one day is over. She hasn't returned so I can be Sayil's sacrifice. Why do you think that is?"

"She means to have Layala take her place," I answer, my voice sounding flat even to my ears.

"I know what she is, and what Death's offers mean." He cocks his head, watching me. "You know she can't be trusted."

I nod hesitantly. "Yes." *But I will kill her before she lays a finger on Layala.*

"Three days, that's how long a soul must be dead before they can take on the mantle. That is the time we have."

I nod again, slowly mulling over his words.

I sit and think, my thoughts as tired as my body. I feel sluggish, like my mind can't keep up with my grief. But then I decide on something; I don't know if Rami could have stopped Layala, I don't know why he didn't come to me immediately, but I *do* know that I can use him to bring Layala back.

"I will do it," I say finally, and though I struggle to meet Rami's eyes, I force myself to. "I will need the girl's body and soul, but I will do it." I set Illyas's soul seed on the shelf beside Layala's and turn to face Rami. He's standing right behind me, so quiet I didn't even sense his presence.

"Sorry to startle you," he says with a small smile. He's eyeing me sharply, like he knows something but isn't saying, but I push the suspicion away. He is nervous, like I am.

I wave him off. "We need to go into Death now, then. It may take a while, though. I haven't been able to get in as easily—"

"No worries, Hakawati. I have a little death realm magic of my own."

He reaches out his hand to me, and I take it. "The nearest cemetery is right behind here, no?"

I nod, and he leads me behind the cottage. We settle down atop a grave, and Rami gives my hand a squeeze.

"Waste no time, Hakawati, when we are in. Not even to see Layala."

My heart aches at his words, but I nod.

Soon, I will have all the time in the world with my Layala by my side once again.

26

WE'RE IN DEATH NOW, AND Rami is ahead of me. I try to keep up, but I'm so, so tired, and my emotions are strained.

You'll have Layala back soon. You'll have Layala back soon.

"Do everything I tell you, when I tell you, as I tell you," Rami directs as he outlines the air before us in the shape of a door. "Your soul will take on some substance once it gets near to the Waiting Place. You will feel pain, you can be injured, and all that can affect whether you can resurrect people in life. Understood?"

I nod as a door appears, its stone doorway crumbling, its wooden face rotted through. Even its handle is rusted and falling off.

"How do you have this magic?" I say.

"I told you, I have a bit of death magic in me."

"But—"

"We don't have time for questions, Hakawati."

I step back from the door, then peer around it. It looks as if it is floating in the air, empty beyond its crumbling face.

"There's nothing behind it," I say. The knob creaks, the door opening under my touch. The sound is sharp in the stillness of death, and I hear the rustling of creatures coming out to look.

"This will take us to the Waiting Place," Rami says, "Hurry, go through."

He takes my hand, and under his breath, chants an old verse.

Kan ya ma kan,

Al-qasas zaman,

Ya warat tafah,

Adamah al-dinya

Dem al-alam

Fatayh al-bab

Fatayh al-mote

Sakaer hiyat

Fatayh al-rouh

"Repeat it with me," he says without glancing at me.

We repeat the chant, line by line, my voice ringing after Rami's. Our fingers hover over the door's wood; our bodies fading.

"Feel it?" he asks.

"I feel . . . sick."

"That's your life draining from you," he explains. "Some life has to die to open death. Death is a taker, not a giver. And whatever it takes, it never returns."

I notice him fading, his skin and blood unstitching themselves, becoming more ephemeral. I look down at my own body, watching it dwindle into grays and whites and blues as pale as the dreariest sky.

"This part of death is less kind than what you've seen before," he says.

I snort. "I don't think I've even seen much of anything nice."

Rami fades then, only a limn of light silhouetting him giving evidence of his form.

And then we're in the outskirts of the Waiting Place.

It feels different here, more sluggish, less inviting than before. This part of death I always avoided because it was the closest to Jahannam.

"It's so cold," I say, my teeth chattering. I rub my hands up and down my arms, but my blood is sluggish and my translucent skin looks blue and paper-thin.

"We can't spend too much time here," Rami says. "Frostbite."

I follow him down a tunnel made of ice and smoke, the only thing in this part of death. The tunnel stretches on, leading past Jahannam's borders and more into the middle part of death, the Waiting Place. But it also forks to the right, curving around the Waiting Place, leading closer to Mote's gates.

"This is the path we're taking. It's the easiest way to get to Mote without being dead yourself," he says.

We continue down the tunnel until we reach the forked path.

"This way," he says as a honey-scented wind wafts toward us.

I sniff, recognition washing over me. "Souls," I say. "Happy souls."

But Rami scoffs. "Pay attention to your surroundings. Death is beguiling and lulls you into inattention. That's how you get stuck," he says.

He steps in even closer now, so close that I almost feel his skin against mine, even though I know it's my imagination.

We take the forked path, the ice and smoke tunnel morphing into a vine and thorn and flower bridge. A smooth river runs underneath it, the waters silver and blue.

"Step carefully," he says. "See those gaps between the vines and branches?" He points at our feet. The bridge is made of intertwined vines, but they're not tight enough to be seamless. "If your foot gets stuck, you'll get cut up on the thorns."

I step gingerly on the vine bridge, testing my weight.

I let him go ahead of me, but stay close behind, watching carefully in case he falls. Not that I could do anything if he did. The bridge is long and canopied with colorful flowers and leaves, the only color against the gray of death in this area.

"Don't be fooled," Rami calls back, as though reading my mind. "Some of those flowers are poisonous."

I shoot my head up to look at them.

"Don't jostle the plants," he continues. "So the petals don't fall on you."

The bridge sways gently under our feet, but I know one shift in our weight to either side could flip the bridge out from under us into the river below.

Rami points to a tree so high I have to crane my head to see its top, and still I see no end to its height. "See that tree there? That's the tree of death. Its roots run deep into the belly of death; they travel into Jahannam, into Mote, and touch almost every part of death. Once we get to that tree, we're at Mote's borders."

Before long, our fingers are grazing the tree of death. Its bark is rough, pockmarked and wrinkled from age.

"It feels . . . I can feel it humming," I say, my fingers pressed against its trunk.

"Follow this root to Mote," Rami says, gesturing at a root thicker than my thighs pressed together.

We follow its curving path through woods of muted greens and browns and greys. The woods are in the likeness of one in life, but more faded. The animals move more slowly, the birds flying as if through honey, the ground animals hopping and running as if through syrup. Even larger animals, ones hunters in life would take home as trophies, move as if their energy has been sapped out of them.

And it has—death takes all it can and leaves little behind. The more time spent in death, the more death takes from you.

"Come, Hakawati, move quicker."

I quicken my pace, and though my muscles burn with the effort, I don't let up.

"Turn left," he says, when we get to where the root forks. "Left to Mote's gates, right to death's sea."

I do as he says, my feet sinking into wet moss. The moss is muted greens and brown, a few purple and blues, and one large red patch.

"See the red moss against that rock?" he says, pointing. "Turn to the left there." As we do so, he points his finger ahead of us and says in a hushed voice, "Here we are."

I straighten and follow his gaze. Two columns stand feet apart from each other, bars in between. A low wall juts from either side of the columns, stretching out as far as I can see.

"Mote's Gates," I say, feeling wonder even through my grief. "We're really here."

27

SEVEN GUARDS STAND AT ATTENTION before the gate. Their faces are frozen, as are their bodies. But their chests rise and fall in slow, shallow breaths that let me know they're alive—or as alive as they can be, living in death.

"They're not truly asleep," Rami says. "They're just as aware as you and me. Any hint of trouble, they'll awaken." He pauses before them, head tilted. "Tell them a story," he says. "Tell them a story to pay your way through the gates."

I glance away from the guards to the jinn. "Any story?"

"Any story."

I screw my eyes shut and open my mouth to tell a tale.

There was a lion who lived in the desert and who ate a jewel. That jewel was as large as its head, as red as the burning sun, and as hard as the mountain stone.

This lion ate the jewel, breaking it into pieces with its strong jaws, cracking through it with its powerful teeth. And when the jewel lay in pieces in the sand, the lion swallowed each piece whole, feeling their weight settle in his stomach.

A hunter watched the lion and knew the wealth it carried in its belly. This hunter was a greedy hunter, and he was as fearless as he was greedy.

He stalked the lion for days, waiting for the right moment to bring it down and gut it. The day came when the lion settled in for a nap in the shade of a palm tree near a desert oasis. The oasis wasn't much, just a shallow dip in the sand that filled with the odd rain that showered the desert.

The lion wasn't stupid, though, and knew the hunter was following him. He kept one eye open just enough that he could see the hunter stalking toward him. The hunter came from behind, but the lion was positioned so he could watch the hunter's reflection in the water.

Just as the hunter raised his arrow to shoot the lion in the back, the lion roared and bellowed, and leapt up, swiping the hunter with its sharp claws.

The hunter's belly was shredded into ribbons, and blood poured out of him. He curled up tight in the sand like a child in its mother's womb. As the blood dried from his body in the sharp desert heat, it hardened over his skin, and the man became a jewel as large as the lion's head and as bright as the burning sun and as hard as the moutain stone. The lion swiped at the jewel and gnawed on it, breaking it into pieces. The lion then swallowed each piece, and when he was done, he went to the oasis and lapped at the water. With his belly full, he settled in for a proper nap under the palm tree he so loved.

The guard blinks, his frozen body melting into flesh and flowing blood. He blinks again and yawns, stretching his arms above his head as he turns a sharp gaze on me. My breath hitches in my throat and I think I've made a mistake. *Did I hear this tale from elsewhere? Have I seen it before, when passing souls through?* "*Ahlan wa sahlan,*" the guard says, then steps aside, unlocking the gate for me. *Welcome.*

I look back at Rami, who gives me a sharp nod before stepping up to another guard. He opens his mouth and tells his own tale.

There was a man and a woman, married for years, who were wise to believe in the evil eye. They knew spirits made of smoke, not flesh, roamed the earth, looking for ways to cause mischief.

The man's name was Pot, and the woman's name was Kettle. They both wore small blue beads on their clothes to protect them from the evil eye, which was the magic of the spirits, but could be cast by unwitting humans with ill, or at least, unkind, intention.

One day, the man grew tired of his wife's talking and wished her to stay silent. The woman was hurt her husband did not want to listen to her and felt lonely as she drew water from their deep well.

A jinn by the name of Breekh was passing by the well, invisible to the human eye.

After a while of silence, the woman continued her story, trying to get her husband's attention. But the husband, who wanted nothing but silence, cursed out at his wife, "Ya nan al Breekh!" he said. "Damn you, Breekh!" And in that moment, the man cast the evil eye on his wife without knowing it. Breekh, the jinn, heard this, and thus he was summoned.

The man did not know why he had called out Breekh instead of his wife's name, but he ignored the thought and sat brooding on why he'd married this woman in the first place.

What the man and woman didn't know, though, was that in the jinn language, Breekh meant Kettle.

"It was her beauty," he thought. "Her beautiful mouth blinded me to the tongue inside it. If I had known I would know no silence, I'd have never married her. What I wouldn't do for silence."

The jinn stole the wife away from the man, forcing her into a world made of fire and smoke and ash. A world where the earth erupted in plumes of flames and spewed molten rock on cities far below the fiery mountain.

The jinn locked the woman in the belly of the mountain, leaving her to sweat and her body to shrivel in the heat.

The man cursed himself for his foolishness, and he called upon the old sheikhs, who drew on their powers against the evil eye. And though the woman noticed the blue bead she wore glowing, the spell would not break. Breekh held her captive for years, until Kettle became the molten earth itself. She became the fiery mountain, and that is why the great mountain in the distance is called the Kettle of Fire.

The man lived his days in solitude, but they were not peaceful ones. He was lonely and missed the sound of his wife's voice. He cursed himself until his dying breath for giving up the one person who loved him enough to want to talk to him.

The guard blinks, scowls, but then steps aside. "Ahlan wa sahlan."

Rami gestures at me to follow him as we step through the gates of Mote and into the heart of death.

"This will lead us to the holding waters," he says, "in Earth's realm."

"Earth?" I repeat. "Mother Earth?"

Rami nods, his mouth set in a grim line. "That is where Kamuna keeps Sayil's body and seed."

28

HE LEADS ME THROUGH PARTS of death I've never been in, parts I am cut off from being only Hakawati.

How does a jinn boy like him travel through more of death than a Hakawati like me?

I feel my suspicions against him rise up, and I wonder, *What isn't he telling me?*

But Rami continues leading me on through the area. Through parts that are filled with colors more hazy than rich-bodied. The air is still, more like a weight, and I feel we are moving through pomegranate molasses. With every breath I take, I taste a rich sweetness on the back of my tongue, but it's followed by a slight rot, as if the sweetness is trying to mask it.

And when I look down at my feet, there's sand. I walk ahead, my feet kicking up dust and sand the color of an orange rind.

"Where is this?" I ask.

"Bab al-Sahra," Rami says. "Desert Gate."

The breeze here coats sand all over my skin and forces me to squint my eyes to keep grit from getting into them. I want to say something, but I'm afraid sand will clog my throat. I'm holding my arm up to my face now, trying to protect my mouth and eyes and nose. But it settles in my ears, sitting on my eyelashes, clogging my throat.

I cough and sputter and try to spit out the sand in my mouth. I can feel its graininess, like I'm chewing through rubble.

"Ah," Rami mutters, just as the wind dies down. I blink a few times and rub grit out of my eyes. We're in a tunnel now, made of glass and vines and wood. Beyond the glass, the sand is still whipping about, but nothing touches me.

Hanging every few feet from the vines and wood are small orbs caked with sand.

"Take a bite when you find a red one," he tells me.

As I pass under one of the white fruits—I guessed they were a fruit of some kind—sand crumbles off its face, revealing a thick red skin underneath.

"Pomegranates."

"Fruit of life" he says. "These are Sahra Pomegranates. Without them, you can't enter the Sahra realm."

Rami takes one, brushing sand from its face. He slices the skin with a long, sharp fingernail, then pulls out a handful of seeds and presses them against my forehead. "This will be the mark that lets you past the gate. Eating the seeds also helps protect your own soul from deteriorating. Make sure to eat as much as your stomach can hold." I feel juice from the seeds run down my forehead and drip off my nose, and I wipe at it, drinking some of the liquid off my finger.

I stop walking. "Wait," I say, the pomegranate weighing heavy in my hand.

He pauses and cocks his head at me.

"Sand," I say, more to myself. "Pomegranates. I know the story. Or parts of it, really."

Earth fashioned a being made of clay and sand and made golems.

Sea made a creature of salt and water and made marids.

Sky took air and cloud, wisps and rain, and made ghouls.

Fire took ash and smoke and made jinns.

"We are going to see Earth herself," I muse.

"She is older than the earth, but she is Earth, yes."

"She created golems," I add. "To help."

Rami scowls. "She did, yes, long ago. But since then, she has done very little for anyone or anything but herself."

"What do you mean?" I begin, but he cuts me off by slicing his hand through the air.

"That story is not your concern, Hakawati. All you need to do is tell your little stories. No more, no less, and only when the time comes."

I close my mouth and say nothing as he leads us through the tunnel.

Keep quiet, Hakawati. Just keep quiet, don't upset him, and keep your head level. I want to tell him that I am Hakawati, that I have been telling the stories of the dead for years, and that these stories aren't little stories, as he calls them. They are the tales the dead pay to get through Mote.

Instead, I shove more of the pomegranate seeds into my mouth to keep from talking, dropping pieces of the thick peel behind me as I walk.

"Here we are," he says, pausing before a door. It's also glass, but I can't see through it to what's behind. He raps his knuckles twice on the door and steps back.

A small creature, no taller than my knees, opens the door. It's made of clay, alive as much as Saqr ever is when I've animated him.

"Ahlan, Ahlan," the golem says to us both as it steps aside to let us through, a false smile on its face. "Mother's been expecting you to show up. Though I don't think she's happy."

29

THE GOLEM LIMPS AHEAD, ONE foot dragging slightly behind as he leads us through a clay garden. It's filled with statuettes of animals, creatures, plants. None I've seen or heard of before. A fountain made of clay rises in the center, its center column spouting water. The water mixes with raw mud, leaving a pool of wet clay behind, waiting to be molded into something.

"She likes pottery," Rami states matter-of-factly, as he gestures around us.

"I always wondered where jinn clay magic came from."

"Jinn are forged from fire, and so are clay beings," he says. "And ash is of the earth, so jinn and golem both come from the earth itself, though in different ways."

I nod, running my fingers down one of the arms of a statue of three women. The women are joined at their backs, though they each have their own set of limbs. Each woman's face holds a different expression, one wide-eyed in fear or shock, another's lips downturned in a scowl, the last, her hands clasped tight over her mouth, as if muffling a scream.

"Her sisters," Rami says, when he notices my gaze lingering on the three women. "There were four earth sisters, one to rule each season. Mother Earth turned the other three into clay and took over all seasons."

"Why?"

He shrugs. "Why does Mother Earth do anything? Why does she cause floods and lightning, thunder and volcanoes? Earthquakes, monsoons? She does because she can."

I hold back a shiver and hurry my pace behind the golem, wanting to get out of the garden now.

"Why ask *her* for help?" I question. "You can't trust a woman who turned her sisters into statues."

"I can trust her *power*," he says, "and that's good enough for me."

The golem swings open a clay door and steps aside to let us into a glass greenhouse. Vines are curled against the glass panes of the walls and ceiling, leaves sprawling all around. It smells like wet earth and scented petals, like grass in the early morning still wet with dew, and even of sunshine. But there's something else under it all, a sort of rawness, like meat I buy from the butcher, still red with blood. The air is heavy and cloying, and I taste metal in the back of my throat.

I sweat as the golem leads us through, and the sensation that the plants are closing in tighter creeps up on me. I want to slice at them, to hold them back, but I have no blade on me. And even if I did, I'm not sure the plants wouldn't fight back. So instead, I keep my arms lifted from my sides to create more space around my torso and follow the golem.

"Gall," a woman's voice calls out. I hear snipping, as of scissors, and the crack of thin branches.

"Yes, Mother," the golem calls out, hurrying off and leaving us behind.

He reappears a moment later, though, and gestures at us to hurry behind him.

The leaves are wider here, as big as my head, or bigger, and they hang from vines and stems as thick as my forearms. Some of the stems are only as wide as my thumb, but I can still imagine someone wrapping them around a neck and . . . but I shake my head of the thought.

What is wrong with me?

"I felt you eat my fruit," a woman's voice says. The golem holds back a few leaves to create a path for Rami and me. We pass through, and the golem lets the leaves fall like curtains behind us. It's a bit darker here, the foliage pressing around and above us.

A woman stands with scissors in her hands, clipping at plants and branches. I notice pockmarked areas of her skin, as if small fruit, like berries, were plucked right from her flesh.

She glances up at me, her eyes boring into mine. "Who is this?" she asks, taking a step closer as she snips at the air with her scissor blades.

"Hakawati jinn," Rami says, stepping around me, as if to protect me from Earth's blades. "She's a friend of mine."

His voice is weaker, as if words are getting caught in his throat. I've never seen him frightened like this before, even with Kamuna, and my blood runs cold and sluggish in my veins.

"A friend?" Earth says, closing her blades with a single sharp snip. She tucks the scissors tip-down into a belt at her waist and steps forward again. "Those are hard to come by, especially in these times. Enemies, though," she says with a long breath, "those are more fruitful."

Rami bows his head slightly, as if in acknowledgement of what Earth has just said. I don't mirror him but stare at the woman with the leaves caught in her thick hair, the tattoo of ferns and vines running up and down her bare skin. Her face is tanned by the sun, her eyes as green as moss. Her hair is as brown as tree bark. Twigs stick up out of the strands. But the twigs are intentional, thin but strong, and holding her hair back in a loose, low bun.

"What is it you want?" Earth asks.

"I need to pass through your realm to the holding waters," Rami says.

Earth slits her eyes at me. "And this one. Why is she here?"

"The holding waters have Death's daughter in it," I start.

Earth sighs and glances up to the glass ceiling of the greenhouse. "Once again, jinns prove themselves to be more trouble than they're worth." She levels her gaze at me. "Then what do you need me for?" Her voice is languid, as if bored by the conversation.

"To let us through," Rami says.

"And what do I get for it?"

He squeezes his eyes shut for a moment. "Please, just let us through."

Earth draws her eyebrows together. "The waters are mine, and everything in them are mine."

"Please," Rami repeats. "Let us through."

"I didn't raise your annoying little clay family when you asked me to, or even demand that Death do so, and yet you think I would allow you into my realm?" Earth says, then snorts. "Why would I help you now?"

"Please," he says yet again, so weak I bend my head closer to hear.

Earth shrugs and moves to prune more of her plants.

I notice Gall, the golem, standing with his eyes to his feet.

"Let us through," I tell him under my breath.

But he either doesn't hear me or pretends not to.

Earth snaps her fingers at Gall. "Get rid of these pests from my realm."

"We're jinns," I say. "We're no more trouble than we need to be. I want to raise my child from the dead and Rami here wants to raise his family."

Earth blinks once, then throws her head back and laughs. Her neck is ruddy, lined with dark veins that look like smudges against her skin. "I don't do anything for free."

I glance at Rami, who's standing too still.

"We only want—"

"Want, want, want. All anyone comes to me for is something they want. Well, what *I* want is to have you out of my realm."

"My child is dead!"

"So?" Earth's voice is thick, as if clogged with dirt. "Things live, things die. That is the way."

"She's young," I argue.

"So are saplings, so are the seeds they grow from, the leaves in the spring, so are the dew drops that die as the sun climbs the sky. All things are young at one point."

"She won't grow old. She is dead and will stay dead if I don't—"

"What makes her life more valuable, jinn, that you would seek to command me in my own realm?"

"She is my daughter."

"And she is nothing to me. Just as you are."

I try again. "Rami needs your help."

"I've said no," Earth says and turns her back on me.

"We will owe you a favor," I offer.

She snorts.

"Please," I say. "Rami's—"

"—my son, you little jinn fool."

30

Rami refuses to meet my eyes.

My body goes rigid, as if rooted to the ground. "I . . ." I begin. "He's your son?"

Earth turns around to face me with a smirk. Rami still doesn't look at me.

"I thought you drowned all of your children when they were born," I say to Earth. "The stories all say—"

"I kept that one," Earth interrupts, glaring at Rami. "His father was jinn. I thought he might be useful. He's proven himself not to be," she adds with a sigh, spoken more to herself than to us.

"He means nothing to you, then," I say.

Earth shrugs. "Nothing and everything." Her voice is callous, uncaring.

"But you care for him?" I point out. "You're his mother."

"Not more than I would for a sapling pushing through winter's snow. I want it to succeed, but I won't lift a hand to help, unless I'm in the mood."

"Please," I say. "I only want my daughter back, and Rami wants his family. His father's family," I add.

"And I only want the earth to set ablaze and start anew," Earth snaps. "We don't always get what we want. But in my realm," she pauses, eyes narrowing. "I do get what I want. And I want you both gone."

"Lead them out of my realm," she says with a snap of her fingers at Gall. "And don't let them back in."

"Mother," Rami says. "It's my family, and my cousins, and—"

"*Your* family, jinn, not mine."

"Yes, *my* family. Blood."

Earth shrugs again.

"Please," I beg. "Let us through and we won't ask any other favors of you."

Earth stares at me and for a breath, a delirious breath, I think she is going to relent.

"No."

31

"Why didn't you tell me she is your mother?" I say to Rami when Gall throws us out and slams the gate on us. "Why hide that from me?"

Rami's face hardens and he purses his lips. "She is less a mother to me than a clump of dirt in human form could be. She is nothing to me, and I am nothing to her."

"But she is your mother."

"And the only thing she passed on to me was some of her death magic."

I want to reach out to him, offer him something of a mother's touch, but I know it would never be the same as his true mother. *And this is why he wants to become Death. Because his own mother turned his back on him, wouldn't even lift a finger to help him. The poor boy thinks this is his last resort. And he may be right.*

"Earth," I begin, "she has . . ."

He gives me a look that tells me to stop talking about her.

I frown but decide not to press him. "The holding waters," I say instead. "They become a river in life, and in death?"

Rami interrupts. "We can get to the holding waters another way. A longer way, and far more dangerous, but it might work." He nods to himself then says, "Follow me, Hakawati. We're going to the river that flows through death."

We've returned to the split road we'd been on earlier. "Follow it to the bend, then continue on until the river runs red, then black, then silver. The silver are the holding waters," Rami says, gesturing at a silvery boat half-tucked on the river's bank. My limbs feel languid, my thoughts sluggish. It takes all I have to put one foot before the other. But I move toward the boat, keeping one eye on Rami.

The boat looks scraped, as if it's been struck with swords and blades, and I run my fingers over its surface, feeling the deep grooves. It's glass, I realize, not silver, and I can see through its bottom into the murky river below. The waters churn and splash over the boat's edge. Realization hits me. The grooves aren't blade marks; they're claw marks.

"And creatures?" I say. "They live in the waters. How will I defend against them?"

"You won't. You'll let them be, and they'll let you be in return," Rami says, his expression grim.

"And if something happens?"

He shrugs. "Don't worry so much, Hakawati. You—and the boat—will be fine."

His words slam into me. "Me? You mean *we.*"

"Eh, well." Rami scrunches his face. "You've heard of Nahr?"

"The river witch?"

"The one and only," he sighs. "She and I, well, we don't get along. And if she sees me, she might try to drown me—and anyone else in my company." He holds up a hand. "Please don't ask for the story. Just go, retrieve Sayil, and return to me in one piece. I'll wait here for you."

I narrow my eyes at him, wondering, *Is this a trick?*

But what trickery would this be, and why? What does he have to gain by harming me now? If Layala remains dead, she takes on Death's mantle, Rami won't get it for himself, and then where would he be?

I shake my head to clear the thoughts. *Keep your head straight, Hakawati. And swallow your suspicions for now; they'll only distract.*

Rami helps me into the boat. He stretches a leg out to push the boat forward. Water sloshes at my feet, but the boat seems strong and sturdy, at least for something in death.

"Watch the bends," he says, cupping his hand over his mouth against the rushing waters. "They can be quite choppy."

But his words are snatched by a wind, and I only hear part of it before I understand what he was saying.

I hold on tight to my oars and guide the boat down death's river.

I've been meandering down the river for maybe a half hour, I think. I almost want to relax my shoulders; the ride has been smooth. But I know death has a way of lulling you before luring away your soul. I'm nearing the river's bend now, though, and water mists onto my face, into the boat, swirling at my feet.

I tighten my grip on the oars and force the boat into a steadiness I don't feel.

The river swirls around me, under me, and as I near the bend, it spins me around. The boat cracks against rock but doesn't shatter.

My arms are strong with fear as I force the boat around with oars and steady it forward. The bend isn't as sharp as I thought it would be, but not soft enough for my lack of boat skills.

The river itself is speckled with red, like a mottled bird's egg. As the current carries me ahead, the speckles coat more of the water's surface, melding into a skein.

It's the red river, the blood river, and just as I think it, the air grows heavy with the metallic tang of blood. It soaks the air, hangs like a heavy curtain around me. I gag on it, but even as I hold my breath, I taste metal and salt deep in the back of my throat. So much salt, I screw up my face and spit into the water, trying to get the taste off my tongue.

Water—blood—sprays across my face and hands. I rub the drops off, but only end up smearing it across my skin, like oils applied to a freshly dead body, oils that never absorb, only sit atop dead skin.

A figure rushes under the boat's glass bottom, a dark shape cutting through the blood under my boat. I make out pale skin, like the underbelly of a fish, and seaweed hair. It cuts ahead of me, to the side, and rises from the water. Nahr, the river witch, watches me slit-eyed, red blood dripping from her hair down her shoulders.

She raises a hand to me, an acknowledgement, before she slips back under the water.

The blood calms now, no longer spraying into my face, as the boat continues ahead. It seems idyllic, and because of that, my body coils tighter, my grip on the boat enough to turn my knuckles white.

I don't trust the calm.

The air turns to a sweet decay, and I gag and retch on it. It's the smell of flesh rotting under earth, under leaves and flowers. The river turns black and sludgy, blood becoming rot. I shrink into myself in the boat, trying not to be touched by the water.

Nahr appears once again, now on the river's bank, twining long river plants together into rope. She ties the cords together into a ring, one end dangling free.

I set my eyes straight ahead, not making contact with the river witch. But even as I pass her, I can imagine that rope tugging on my neck, tightening, straining against flesh, if I had any in this realm. I choke and force myself to breathe in, out, in, out. The forced breathing calms me, and it's soon enough that the water melds from black into silver.

Small fish with feathers for fins and pebbles for eyes swim around the boat. They curl up around one another, chasing each other's tails. I hear them yipping, as if laughing, at their carefreeness.

A few leap out of the water, within fingers' reach. But I don't reach out to try to touch one. I'm sure their teeth are as sharp as jagged bone.

The boat slows, as if steadied by an unseen hand. It curves toward the river's bank and lands on it, jerking me forward, as if trying to spit me out as soon as it can.

I stumble to the bank, setting the oars aside in the boat, though I wonder if they could serve as weapons. Silver water laps at my feet. Ahead there's a cliff, a bone-white path cut through it. I follow the path with my eyes up the cliff, where it disappears into a speck at the top.

I know of that smoking cliff, with fire and molten rock under its surface. It's small, much smaller than others of its kind. Smoke curls from its mouth, like from a chimney atop a house. There's the story that speaks of it, of the man who cursed his wife and was stolen by a jinn after. But the story means nothing right now, and I ignore it, focusing instead on the river.

I turn and follow the riverbank. There's a shimmering far ahead of me as the bank curves around the cliff's base. The shimmering is water, a small pond with a tree bent over it, like a mother over a child.

It's to this pond I make my way.

32

THE SHIMMERING IS BECAUSE OF white flower petals dusted from the tree. The petals float like corpses in the pond, their faces pale, waiting to be plucked from the water. I notice a broken branch, torn from the trunk like a shoulder severed from its socket.

But it's not white I'm looking for; it's red. A red pomegranate seed. And a girl's body.

I dip my hands into the water and push aside the petals to see. The flowers float back together, and I shove more aside, trying to find Sayil's seed.

"She's deep in the waters," a voice whispers behind me.

I jump, startled.

It's Nahr again.

She's on dry land now, her legs long and slim, like a frog's. They're a pale green, as if she smeared moss over herself and let its moisture color her skin. She's smiling at me, but it's not friendly. It's calculating. Her head is cocked to the side, slitted eyes watching me.

She shuffles over, and I notice the top halves of her thighs are fused together and her bare feet are webbed. She kneels by the pond's edge and dips a finger into the water. "Deep," she says. "At the bottom. *She* put it there."

I don't have to ask her who she means.

I try to look through the petals, to gauge the water's depth. But I'm sure I could swim and swim and not reach the pond's bed.

"Could you get it for me?" I ask. "The soul seed and the body?"

Nahr cocks her head again, sizing me up. "Maybe," she says.

I sigh, looking up at the gray sky rather than the water witch. "What's the favor?"

She grins, exposing two rows of pointed teeth. "Bring back someone for me."

"Who?"

"A sister," she says, stretching out each letter.

"What sister?" I ask. "Bring her back from where?"

"She is dead, but I froze her. Her body is without rot." Her grin slips off her face like oil on water. Nahr points at the pond. "This was hers. And my other Sisters'."

"The pond was your sister's?" I say. "What happened to her, then?"

"Earth."

"Earth killed her?"

Nahr nods. "The dirt hag wanted it, and she kills when she wants things. Earth killed Sister. A branch fell on her." She points at the broken branch I noticed before.

I think for a breath. "So, the holding waters, this pond, wasn't Earth's. It was your sister's?"

Nahr nods again. "But," and she grins once more, and that dark, calculated look returns to her eyes, "my Sisters and I will take revenge. Not today, not tomorrow, but . . ." She nods as she speaks, as if agreeing with herself. "We will."

"If," I say, "if you get me Death's daughter's soul seed and her body, I will bring your sister back to life."

"And tell her story," Nahr says. "To keep her soul strong."

"If I tell her story, she will pass to Mote," I start, but Nahr shakes her head.

"Old folk—us—the ancients, we do not die like you do. We are older even than any Death that has ever lived." Her voice is hoarse and strained, as if being out of the water this long dries out her throat. "We . . . die . . . in our own way."

"So Earth," I say, "she isn't—"

Nahr is shaking her head before I'm done speaking. "She is too old to die. She is of the world itself. She will die when the world itself dies or something powerful destroys her. She is . . . in between."

I nod, though I'm not sure I understand her.

Nahr slips one foot into the pond, then another. She is sitting on its bank now, water up to her ankles.

"I will bring them to you," she says, "but you promise."

I hold a hand to my heart and bow my head slightly. "Favor for a favor," I say.

She nods once, then slips her lithe, green body into the water and disappears under the curtain of petals.

I circle the pond three, six, seven, nine times, and still Nahr hasn't returned.

I chew on my lip, chew on my cheek, then pluck at the white flowers, tearing them into little pieces before sending them scattering on the wind.

"Nahr?" I call, bending over the pond's surface, searching for the slitted eyes and wild hair.

But I don't see the water witch.

I consider slipping into the water myself, but if the water witch can't manage, how would I? Was I foolish to come here? To try to control death beyond my jinn magic?

What if she lied? The river water witch lied, didn't she? She must have.

My heart freezes. *What if she is with Earth? What if she went to tell her I am here?*

I pace around the pond again, two, three more times. I take hold of the branch skimming the surface, sinking it into the water, testing the depth again. But the waters are deep, so deep, and I'd drown before I touched the bottom.

She's lied, hasn't she?

Sayil's seed, where could it be? Shouldn't it float? Shouldn't her body float?

How could I have been so stupid? Why would anything sink so deep in a pond? They should have been floating, right at the top where I could pluck them out.

And then I think, *What if something's gone wrong? What if the witch didn't lie? What if she herself drowned in those dark, deep waters?*

I brush aside flower petals with the tip of the branch, trying to see into the waters. But the pond is too dark, too deep, for me to see anything. I look for bubbles, for ripples, for *anything* to let me know the water witch is still there.

After a few more breaths pass, I slip off one shoe, then turn to slip off the other. I slide one leg, then the other into the pond, the water icy and seizing me immobile for a breath, two breaths, until I force my limbs to move. I take a deep breath, and just as I sink down, a green head breaks through the pond's surface, a fist outstretched.

I sputter to the surface as a strong grip clasps my shoulder.

It's Nahr, and she holds out her free fist to me. Her skin is paler, and she's shaking.

"Nahr?" I say, my teeth chattering too. She pulls me out of the pond and lays me on the bank.

She unfurls her fingers. In her palm is a small red orb.

I pluck it from her, my fingers already blue, hands shaking from cold. "And the girl? Sayil's body?"

She shakes her head, but then a breath later, she's disappeared under the surface once more.

I clasp Sayils's seed to my chest. *Soon, Layala, soon I can hold you and smell you and keep you safe once again,* I think, wishing I could give her my own heart to bring her back to life at this very moment. But then a dark thought follows. *You've never kept her safe before, why would you now?* I shake my head of the thought and focus on waiting for Nahr to emerge.

It takes longer this time. And when she does surface, she's struggling. I bend over the pond, snatching Sayils's body from her. She's heavy, as if her lungs are laden with water, and my heart seizes as I drag her upward. I touch my hand to her face, finding it smooth and without a hint of rot. She's young, my Layala's age, and if not for her light hair, she could be Layala's sister. Even with the pale hair, the resemblance is there in the curve of the plump cheeks, the small mouth, the strong brows.

Nahr coughs as she struggles onto the pond's bank.

"Come," I say, and offer her a hand. She takes it, and her skin is wet and slimy. I pull her out of the water, droplets sliding off her body.

"Shukran," I say, "for your help."

"Thank me by giving me back my Sister," she says, then shuffles off. I hoist Sayil's body over my shoulder and check that her seed is safe and deep in my pocket, then I follow after Nahr, making my way back to the boat.

At the boat, I tuck Sayil's body in it, and yet again, check that the seed is still in my pocket. It is too precious to risk losing. Then I slip back into the boat. Before I've lifted the oars up, Nahr is pushing me back into the water.

"Go," she says. "Be quick about it. I want my Sister back."

The boat casts off on a wind I don't feel. I fall back into my seat, clutching the oars.

Nahr swims alongside me, and I'm sure her arms are pushing the boat along as fast as it can go.

I barely have time to register the smell of rot on the air or the bends of the river before I'm back where I left Rami, though I don't see him anywhere.

"Go," Nahr repeats, and she watches as I leap out of the boat.

"Shukran," I turn to say to her, but she's gone already, leaving behind only ripples where her head just was.

"Rami!" I call out even as I make my way down the riverbank. "Rami!"

He slips out from behind a tree. "I didn't want her seeing me," he says, then peers around me. "Sayil?"

I point at the boat.

Rami pads down to the river and bends over the boat, pulling Sayil's body over his shoulder.

"And her seed?" he asks.

I pat my pocket. "Let's go home."

33

I'M BACK IN LIFE AND the cottage smells of pungent herbs and oil. The smells mask any rot that would be setting into the bodies.

On the table is a bowl of fresh blood and two small red seeds beside it. *Layala's and Sayil's.* I swallow the anger brewing deep within me and instead focus my attention on what I need to do.

Rami left as soon as he set Sayil's body down. "I have to—there are things I want to get in order. I'll bring my family, leave them here," he says. "I'll return shortly . . ." I ignore him and let him leave, focusing instead on the raising.

A little while later, I'm not sure how much time has passed, someone knocks on the door.

"What?" I yell in the door's direction, sharper than I meant. "Who is it?"

I open the door. Silver eyes stare at me.

"Rami," I sigh.

"I'm back. Apologies it took so long."

"Come in and close the door behind you," I say and watch him as he sets the clinking bag of clay figurines down on the table.

"Shay?" I ask. *Tea.* "Maybe something to eat?"

Rami gives a dry laugh. "Feeding me my last meal?"

I don't say anything but set the kettle over the fire. While the tea is brewing, I set a plate of figs and dried apricots on the table. He stares at them but doesn't reach for any.

"Can I help?" he asks when I set the tea before him and he's taken a few sips.

"You can add more wood to the fire."

I rub Layala's and Sayil's bodies with oils and herbs and plait their hair over their shoulders. Rami doesn't say anything, but I hear him scrape back the chair and pull small logs from the corner where I have them stacked.

He throws logs into the grate and lights them, slowly starting the blaze until it's hot enough I have to move away from it.

He's pacing, though, and I hear him muttering to himself. "If you want to do something to burn the energy," I say, "you can bury the sheikh."

I nod my chin at the sheikh's body, lying where I left him.

"I can . . . bury the body."

"In the cemetery, in the back," I say. "I don't want anyone finding him."

"I'll make sure it's a deep hole."

"There's a shovel in the shed, where the tub is. Behind the house. I'll prepare the girls while you do."

I pull the bowl of blood closer to me. The blood is clotted, but I break through it with my finger. I pour oil into the bowls and swirl the blood in it, making it easier to spread over the floor and Layala's body.

She's still coated in the mud and clay from before, but it's hardened now and flaking.

"And I need to get more clay," I tell Rami as he's heading to the door. "And water. Please. Then you can go bury the sheikh."

His footsteps clack against the wooden floor before disappearing outside. He returns a few minutes later with a ball of clay cupped in his palms.

"Leave it there," I say, and he drops it into an empty bowl and pushes it toward me. He leaves, then returns with water sloshing in a bucket and sets it beside me. "And I'll need some of your blood," I say, "to start with."

Rami offers his hand wordlessly and I slice his palm with a blade. I collect the blood in a bowl and slice his other palm, letting the blood fill a second bowl.

"Shukran," I say and hand him clean cloths for his wounds. He leaves, then returns with fresh well water, setting a bucket beside me.

He turns to the sheikh's body and throws it over his shoulder. The door shuts behind him, and I turn back to the girls.

I slice my palm and let myself bleed fresh blood into a bowl.

I coat another layer of clay and water over Layala's body. I rub more oil in, more herbs, and lay more ash over her skin. Then I do the same for Sayil. I dip each of their fingers into my blood and coat their tips. I rub the blood over their mouths and eyes, around the nose, down the front of their necks and across their chests, like a helmet and shield.

Rami returns, and he settles by the table as I finish rubbing another coat of oil over the girls.

"You're preparing both?" he says, surprise making his voice higher.

"I . . . Layala's body should be kept supple," I say, my back still toward Rami. I don't want him to see my face, to catch on to any look of deceit. I don't want him to suspect that I'm about to deceive him.

"But you're raising Sayil, right?" he asks.

I nod, still hiding my face from his view.

"Hakawati," Rami says, his voice sharper now. I turn around to face him. "My sacrifice is for you to raise Sayil."

"I know, Rami, that is what I'm doing."

"I am dying so she can raise my family when she becomes Death."

"Yes, of course," I say through gritted teeth. "I know this."

He stares at me, then flicks his gaze over to the girls. "I'm sorry about Layala, but my sacrifice is for Sayil, and Sayil alone."

I bow my head. "Of course. I'm only keeping her body from rotting quicker."

He gives me a sharp nod of the head, and I turn back to the girls. I set more logs in the fire and make sure the bowls of blood are beside me.

"I'm ready," Rami says behind me.

I turn around. He's standing there, by the table, one hand near the girls' soul seeds, the other holding a knife out to me.

"Please," he says, and his silvery eyes are wide. "Please make it quick. Make it deep." He turns so he's facing away.

I stand behind him, my mouth so dry I pause to drink some water.

"All well?" Rami says, looking at me over his shoulder.

"Yes, yes, of course," I say, and he faces ahead of him again. *This is for Layala. This is for your child. His sacrifice will be worth it. This is for Layala,* I keep repeating to myself.

I settle my hand on Rami's shoulder and force him down to his knees. He's shivering now, his breaths are ragged.

This is for Layala.

I plunge the knife into his neck and watch him bleed.

This is for Layala. This is for Layala. This is for Layala.

He's clutching at his neck, and I resist the urge to place a warm cloth and pack herbs into his wound to stop the bleeding.

"I'm sorry," I tell him, coo to him even, as if he were a child I was putting to sleep. "This will be over shortly."

This is for Layala.

He sputters, and more blood drains out of him. I hold a bowl to capture it, letting the blood fill up, even as Rami slumps to the ground. He's not breathing anymore, and he's still, his eyes closed.

This is for Layala.

I pour both my blood and Rami's together into a bowl and swirl it. I pry Layl's mouth open and slide the blood down her throat.

Then I drink the rest of it.

It's salty and metallic and thick with clot. I gag and choke, and I want to vomit. But I force it down with water, trying not to think too much about it. I hold my fist to my mouth for a few breaths, until my stomach is settled and I know I won't vomit it all out. I set the kettle on to boil, and I eat Rami's soul seed.

I gasp when the soul releases its stories. They're violent and grotesque. Mosaics of body parts and rotting flesh, ash and dust and fire, and death from ages past. I see the rot of decaying bodies choking the earth. I feel the souls not as they were when they died, but before that. They were . . . happy? There is warmth on my skin—sunshine. And I smell fresh grass and rain. I hear music and dancing, the heavy thrum of drumming in the night air.

The images shift, the sounds more distant, and I see dead children. Bodies piled on bodies, then set on fire. The earth spits out fire and flame, and black ash settles on everything. The oceans swallow the ash. I can't make out a single story thread, there are too many scenes flashing before me.

But then my magic settles on one story, and I pluck it out.

A claymaster was married for twenty years to her husband, a painter. She was still young in her own mind, no more than forty years, but she'd never had a child.

She and her husband both wanted children, twins even, so they would always have a playmate in each other.

One day, the claymaster told her husband, "I'm going to make us a child."

Her husband laughed and said, "You can't do that without my help."

"You're right," the claymaster said, and plucked two hairs from the man's head and two from hers. She took two types of clay, one she always used that was easy to mold, and another type that was grainier and took more of her skill to shape.

She mixed both her and her husband's hairs in each of the clay and set about molding both into children.

Two girls, for she'd always wanted a sister, though she only had brothers.

The claymaster shaped them into the most beautiful babies she could—with dimpled cheeks and hands, chubby bellies, bright eyes, and button noses. She molded the clay for days, shaping and drying and heating. Her husband painted the clay, taking weeks to make sure he did his most beautiful work.

Then they waited. They set the clay babes under the light of a full moon, smoothed the bodies with oils and herbs, and splashed a life spell over the clay, given to them by a witch who lived deep in the woods.

The claymaster and her husband went to sleep and prayed their efforts would reward them.

When they awoke to bright sunshine, the claymaster rushed out of her house to check on the clay. In place of what she and her husband left out the night before were two bone and blood babies, smiling up at her as if they'd known her their entire short lives.

"Husband!" she yelled. "Husband, come quick!"

Her husband dashed out of the house, and when he saw the babes, he picked each one up and cried.

"Two girls," the claymaster said, "just as we wanted."

They took the girls inside and raised them in love.

The years flew by and soon the girls were ten and as different as could be. The one fashioned of easy clay was easygoing, with bright blue eyes and pale hair, and her name was Shamsa, the sun. The other was wilder, more stubborn, as if born of the wilderness, with her dark hair and brown eyes, and her name was Amur, the moon. But the two were inseparable.

The claymaster remarked to her husband, "Our girls are so different, perhaps we should separate them, so Amur doesn't spoil Shamsa's goodness."

The two parents thought on it, then decided they would separate the girls, sending Amur to the witch in the woods to keep away from Shamsa, who would stay home with them.

The sisters refused at first, but then when they were asleep one night, the claymaster's husband took Amur, still sleeping, to the witch in the woods and left her at her doorstep. When the witch awoke the next morning, she found the girl still sleeping on a mat of leaves before her house.

"Wake, girl," she said. "You have been deceived, but not by my hand."

Amur was angry, and though she tried, she could not find her way back to her home, and the witch refused to help, saying she did not meddle in the affairs of selfish humans without a good reason. So, Amur stayed with the witch, and she learned the witch's ways.

Years passed, and Shamsa grew more beautiful as Amur grew more wild. But none was less than the other, for they were different sides of the same hand.

One day, Amur spotted Shamsa gathering berries deep in the woods. She was happy to see her sister, but also angry that Shamsa was the one who their parents loved.

So, she decided to kill her and take her place. She followed Shamsa back to their parents' home and learned the route. At night, she waited until all were asleep and snuck into the house, poisoned thorn vine in hand.

But just as she was about to stab her sister in the neck with the thorn, Shamsa's eyes flew open. She recognized her sister instantly, though many years had passed.

"Amur?" she said in a low voice so she wouldn't wake their parents.

Amur's hand dropped and she felt shame for what she had been about to do.

Shamsa eyed the poisoned thorn but drew her sister closer to her. "I wouldn't have blamed you, if you had done it," she said. "Our parents wronged you. I begged them for years to bring you back, but they never listened. Here's what we'll do: you sleep here with me and when they awake, we will surprise them!"

Amur thought on it, then slipped into her sister's bed. They curled up into each other like they did as children and slept as if no years had ever passed between them. When the sun broke through the windows, the sisters awoke and set out a breakfast for their parents, then sat at the table and waited for them to awake.

When the claymaster and her husband awoke, they found both sisters at the table. The claymaster's knees failed her and she fell to the ground. Her husband tore at his hair and asked his deceived daughter for forgiveness.

"You have wronged me," she said. "But I forgive you, for I only want to be with my sister again."

What Amur didn't know, though, was that Shamsa had the poisoned thorn in her hand. With her parents distracted, she rose up and stabbed them both with the thorns, killing them.

"Shamsa!" Amur said. "How could you?"

"They have made my life miserable, from sending you away to keeping me inside the house so no one would spoil me. They are miserable, sorry creatures and didn't deserve the lives they were given."

Though Amur was happy she had her sister back, she knew it was wrong to kill their own parents. Using the witch's magic she learned over the years, she brought the claymaster and her husband back to life. But it wasn't a true life, no, for no witch's magic is stronger than death's. The best she could do was to bring the claymaster and her husband back into the shape of clay dolls. Each full moon, when the clay dolls were set out under the moonlight, they came back to life, just for that night.

And so, the sisters lived this way the rest of their long lives, meeting their parents at every full moon, but living in happiness together the rest of the time.

I'm surprised at the story. It's sweet, even as it came with pain. I hold the story in my mind and quickly write it in blood over Layala's body. I sketch the gardens, the plants, and the witch and Amur and Shamsa, from memory. I write the words of the tale until every inch of her body is covered in it.

"I'm sorry, Rami. And I thank you for your sacrifice," I say aloud. "It will not be in vain."

And if you knew what Layala was planning at the river, if you chose not to stop her, then I care even less for your life. And if you had no hand in this, then know your life goes toward a greater good.

I look down at Sayil, and with as much affection as I can feel for Death's daughter, who looks nothing like my own with her pale hair and pale coloring, yet so similar in her youth and beauty, I say, "I'm sorry, Sayil. But my Layala comes first."

Then I take Layala's soul seed from its jar and eat it.

34

IT DOESN'T FEEL RIGHT. LAYALA'S story isn't what I expect. I know her *feel*, the way her soul felt when she was an infant.

But I shake my head to clear the thought. An infant is not the same as a child is not the same as an adult. An infant barely has stories to their soul, and Layala was far too young when I raised her before. Of course she would feel different.

Still, her story is different, ripe with a grief I know I've had a hand in. It makes my heart bleed, because it's a story I *understand.*

A fisherman lived alone in a hut on a small island of one hundred souls. Every morning, he threw his nets, hoping for a catch that would let him both have a warm meal for the night and something to sell in the market in the morning.

One day, he was out on his boat, his nets cast into the sea. He felt a tug and so went to look to see what was caught in his nets.

He was met with two large eyes and a pleading mouth.

"You are a woman," he said, and lifted the nets out of the water and dragged the woman from its tangles. "Where did you come from?" he asked her.

"From the sea, from deep in the sea," she told him.

"But you are a human woman," he said. "How can that be?"

"I have been cursed by a wicked witch and banished from the sea. She forced me into this skin that breathes the air and not the water I was born in. I was caught in your nets as I was trying to swim to shore."

"Come home with me," the fisherman said. "I will make you my wife and I will offer you safety."

The woman agreed and she went home with the fisherman. The next day, they were wed, and all the people living on the island were invited. There was a meal made of the fish caught by the other fishermen and the spices and herbs their wives grew.

The first year, the fisherman and his new bride lived happily. He took his boat to sea every morning, and she took a long swim and sang to the waters.

But after the first year, the woman grew sad, longing for her family deep under the waves.

"I have to go," she told the fisherman one day. "I don't know when I will return."

"I can't protect you if you leave," he told her.

But she only said, "I will protect myself, and before I leave, I will make sure you are blessed with a catch each morning so you will never grow hungry."

The woman left the fisherman, and for days and weeks, until a year had passed, he mourned her.

On the aniversary of her leaving, the fisherman was out in his boat when he felt a tug in his nets. He glanced over his boat and found his wife caught in them. But her eyes weren't looking at him this time. They were closed and she wasn't breathing.

The fisherman pulled his nets in and cut his wife free. He tried to blow breath into her lungs, tried to warm her with his jacket, but she stayed as still as a rock against pounding waves.

"She is dead!" he cried to the sky. "My beautiful wife is dead. She has drowned in the very sea she so loved."

And so, the fisherman carried his wife back to shore and buried her in a cave where the land and sea kissed. Every night, after he came back from his catch, he visited her, leaving her a bit of his fish as an offering, hoping that one day, through some magic, he would find her again in his nets, her wide eyes staring up at him and a smile on her beautiful lips.

I'm crying at the story, as I feel the pain and longing in it. I swallow the sob of guilt welling up in me, choke back my screams. I touch my child's body and rub my blood all over her again and again. I wash her body with the sacrifice's blood. And I write her own soul's tale over her, sketching the sea, the nets, the fish and the cave the woman was buried in.

I sit back on my heels and survey my child's body, covered in blood and earth and ash. The blood and the stories are intertwined now, the two souls merged. Now all that's left is to let steam enter her nostrils and breathe life back into her body.

35

THIS RAISING TAKES LONGER THAN I expect. When she was an infant, she was raised within half a day. This time, it takes two days and two nights before a finger stirs, as if death is reluctant to give her back.

I don't move from Layala's side, except to get drinks of water and eat a few mouthfuls of food. But I keep vigil at her side, making sure the kettle's steam never runs dry. I hold her hand and wait for her pale white nails to turn seashell pink again. One of her fingers twitches, once, twice, and at first, I think it's just my imagination.

But then it lifts up, and I know the necromancy worked.

"Layl," I say, waving more steam over her face.

I bend over her nose and talk to her, telling her nonsense strings of words, just to get my own breath into her, like she does when she tells stories to her plants in the spring.

"Layl?"

I lay a hand on her chest, waiting to feel that first sharp intake of breath.

"Layl."

I keep repeating her name and rubbing warmth into her arms as I do. Blood is flowing now, color returning to her pale skin. Her touch is warm, too. Her nails are still pale, but less so, almost pink now.

Her eyelids twitch, her eyes darting back and forth beneath them.

"Layl."

She moans, and her arm moves. Once, twice, then she flails one arm over the other and rolls onto her side.

"Layl," I sob. "Oh, Layl. Layl." I crouch over her, wanting to squeeze more life back into her. Instead, I add water to the kettle to create more steam.

I let that steam drift over her, like clouds passing over a mountain.

"Layl."

She moans again, then shifts onto her other side.

Her cheeks are flushing pink now. I check her nails—seashell pink as the day she was born.

"Layl. Open your eyes."

Twitch. Another twitch of the eyelids. Her eyelashes flutter.

And then I see two large dark orbs staring up at me. Layala is alive.

Then, to my surprise, there's a knock on our door.

36

THE KNOCK IS INSISTENT AND reminds me of the guards Abu Illyas sent before.

Layala stirs, moans, and I dart a glance between my daughter's face, the door, and back again.

"Come, Layl, drink some water," I say, holding a lukewarm cup of water to her lips. I don't want cold water shocking her system.

The knocking on the door turns to pounding.

"Coming," I say, trying to force cheerfulness into my voice. But the knocking is too rough, and Layala is still so weak.

I watch her slump back down and curl in toward the fire. Her back seems so small now, shrunken from death, even though I oiled it and kept it from rot with herbs.

I glance through the eyepiece, spotting some men. They knock again, and the door shakes under the force. I swing open the door just wide enough that I could glance around it. "Yes?" I ask.

A dry, veiny hand slaps the door open, but the hinged lock keeps the man from barging in. Still, the hand shoves the door back further until I'm sure the lock will snap.

"Keep out," I say. "My daughter has a contagious fever. And the pox," I add.

The man hesitates, and I see his bright blue eyes trying to look in through the door's crack.

"Open this door, jinn, in the name of town law."

"It's contagious," I repeat.

The man hesitates again, but two others behind him shove him aside and kick at the door. They pound on my door again, and I hear the wood splinter.

"You're going to break my door!" I shout. "And then you will have to deal with Sheikh Hamadi. He bought the door!"

"That's what we're here for, jinn!" the second man says, shoving his face in through the door's gap. "He's dead."

I feign shock, widening my eyes and shaking my head. "What?"

"You heard, jinn, the sheikh is dead. By *your* hand!"

"*My* hand?" I say. "I've been here for days tending to my sick child."

"The servants said they saw you two had an argument."

"When was that?"

"Five days ago."

"And when did the sheikh die?"

The man pauses. "He is missing."

"So, he's missing, not dead," I say.

The man hesitates again. "No."

"You just said—"

"He was known to be coming here," the third man chimes in.

"And he did," I say. "He came to check on his grand-daughter. He saw she was ill, but I told him how contagious she was, so he left."

"You had something to do with it, jinn!" the third man yells. "I know it!"

I try to shut the door and manage to get it almost closed again, though the first man puts a foot in to block it from shutting.

I wish I had that clay wolf, I think.

"Have you sent out a search party?" I ask.

"As we speak," the first man says.

"Then I pray they find the sheikh alive and well, and soon."

"I know you had something to do with it, jinn," the second man says. "I will prove it."

"Prove it if you will," I say, "but the sheikh has not been harmed by my hand." *Thank goodness Rami buried him. Thank goodness Rami buried him. Thank goodness Rami buried him,* I repeat to myself like a mantra. *I just hope they don't search through the cemetery. A fresh grave would be suspicious.*

"She's lying. I know it," the second man adds.

"I am not. And if you don't leave my house right now, I will send ghouls to you and your families."

Their faces blanch. No ghoul would ever be under my command, but the townspeople will believe anything bad about jinn.

"Gh-ghouls?" one of them stammers.

"Yes, ghouls. Death's ghouls. She owes me a favor, and I wouldn't mind calling on it right now," I lie.

The men glance at each other, their eyes wide.

"We'll return, jinn," one says. "With more men and more weapons." He holds up his dagger for effect. "And we will cut down this door and you and avenge the sheikh's death. Mark my words."

I slam the door shut before they can say anything else. I stand there for a moment, resting my head against the thick wood. My hands shake and my body feels jittery.

"Ghouls?" a voice says behind me.

I spin around, bile rising up to my throat.

"Favor?" Kamuna says.

I sigh. "I meant to frighten those men, that's all."

"And so you invoke Death to do so," she says, still smiling. She glances down at Layala, and her smile fades. "Sayil?" she whispers. "What is my daughter's body doing here, Hakawati?"

She leans over Sayil and runs her fingers over the girl's face. "My baby," she moans. "I sensed a raising, but . . ."

She crouches beside Layala. One hand curves around my daughter's arm, rubbing warmth into it. "Hakawati,"

Kamuna says, anger making her eyes blaze. "What have you done?"

I lift my chin. "I raised my daughter from the dead."

"With what sacrifice?" she says, though her eyes drift to Rami's lifeless body on the floor. Her gaze bores into me, and I feel like pushing her out my door and locking it behind her.

Instead, I say, "Rami."

Kamuna stands to her full height and glares at me. "What is going on, Hakawati? Rami was meant to be Sayil's—"

"You never came for him," I say, though I know my argument is weak. "You told him one day, that he would have one day and you would come for him. But you didn't."

"So, you went behind my back and raised Layala."

"You would have made her Death."

"She was dead, Hakawati. And not by my own hand. She was already dead." She glances back down at Layala. "What have you done?"

"I will still raise Sayil," I say. "Just as I promised."

"Promised? Promised!" Kamuna says, pacing the cottage. "I should kill you where you stand. But you're more good to me alive than dead, for now." She pauses in her pacing to jab a finger in my chest. "I could kill her, right here, and pass on my mantle. Then what, Hakawati? All this," she gestures at Layala, still curled up on the floor beside Sayil, "all this would be for nothing."

"I will raise her," I say. "I will raise Sayil."

Kamuna scoffs. "With what sacrifice, Hakawati? You wasted the one sacrifice we had on your daughter." Her voice breaks as she says, "What about *mine*. What about *my* Sayil?"

"I'm sorry," I say, "But my child was dead. I had no choice."

I sit on the ground, no strength left to even keep my shoulders straight. They hunch over and I feel like one of Layala's discarded, broken toys from when she was three or four years old. It was an old wooden thing, with strings attached to its back that she could pull and make it dance with. But she broke the strings, and without them, the toy collapsed, its hinged back no longer upright.

I feel how that toy looked.

Layala moans and stirs, her eyelids still closed.

"Maman?" she says.

I dart to her side, taking her hands in mine. I kiss each finger, feeling how warm and soft they are in my own.

"Oh, Layl, you'll be fine," I say.

"Maman?" she says again, still moaning and thrashing her head side to side. "Maman, the water!" she screams.

"Shhh," Kamuna says the same time I do. We glance at each other, connected in this moment by a mother's bond, then turn our attention back to Layala.

"The river!" she screams, squeezing her hand tight against mine. "I can't breathe!"

"Layl, you're home, you're home here, with me. There is no river, Layl," I try to soothe her.

"Maman! He pushed me!" she screams. And my heart runs cold.

"Who pushed you Layl?" But I'm sure she means Rami.

My daughter's eyes flash open, but she screams the moment they settle on me. Her gaze darts to Kamuna and Layala starts to sob.

"Maman," she says, "who is this woman?"

But she's asking Kamuna, not me.

"Layl," I say, reaching out to her. But she slaps my hand away and crawls into Kamuna's embrace.

"Layala," I begin again.

"Who is Layala?" my child says.

"Layala, *you're* Layala," I say, confused. "Layl."

But Layala is twisting deeper into Kamuna's arms and calling her maman as she sobs.

I reach a hand out to her, but then draw it back. Kamuna is watching me with wide eyes, even as she rocks my daughter in comfort.

"Whose seed did you use, Hakawati?" she says in a low voice.

I swallow hard. "Rami's sacrifice, and-and I used Layl's seed." I point at the table, at the single red seed still there. "That is Sayil's."

"Are you sure? Did anyone come in here between you getting home and raising Layala? Was anyone here?" One of her eyebrows is raised high, as if strung up to her hairline.

I blink once, then twice, before I answer. It's suddenly all so clear. "Rami."

Kamuna's face hardens. "What about him?"

"He did it," I say, and a mirthless laugh slips from my lips. "He did something. He-he must have."

I sit down again, my knees buckling under me.

"He did what, Hakawati?" Kamuna says, still holding Layala.

"I think, I think that jinn switched the soul seeds. He knew, he must have sensed what I was planning." I look up at Layala and reach out for her. She stretches away from me, burrowing deeper into the safety of Kamuna's arms.

Kamuna looks down at Layala, then pulls her back so she can see her face properly. "What is your name, girl?" she asks.

Layala blinks and her face caves in on itself. "Maman, don't you know me?"

"Your name, girl!" Kamuna repeats, harsher than I think she meant to.

"Sayil," the girl says, and my heart shatters into pieces.

There. The truth. Betrayal for my own betrayal. I want to scream, to claw at my chest and rip out my own heart.

I ease away from both Layl, Sayil, and Kamuna and drape myself into a chair.

Kamuna is hugging my—her?—child, hugging the soft warm body I should be holding close to my heart right now.

But the girl is clutching onto Kamuna and letting herself be soothed by Death.

"Hakawati," Kamuna says after a while. "I believe you have raised my Sayil's soul in Layala's body."

"I can see that, Death," I say coldly. I feel more tired than I've ever felt in my life.

Kamuna pulls Layl/Sayil toward me. She kisses the top of Sayil's head, closing her eyes for a breath to take in her scent.

"We need a sacrifice," I say. "To raise Layala. Even if it will be in Sayil's body," I add, choking on the words.

But Kamuna isn't listening to me. She's soothing *Sayil*, Sayil in Layala's body, in *my baby's body*. She glances down at Sayil in Layala's body, and though I'm sure Layala looks nothing like Sayil did in life, Kamuna is holding her gaze with a mother's love. I want to rip them apart and tell her that girl is *mine*, that is *Layala's* body, but I know the soul is Sayil's. The girl is neither daughter and both, all in one.

"I want to hold her," I say, easing myself out of the chair.

But Sayil inches away from me and glances at Kamuna, as if afraid.

"It's alright," Death says. "She won't hurt you."

But Sayil doesn't want to leave her mother's arms, and I just want my child in mine.

"Oh, Layl," I say, moving back to her.

My vision is still blurred, and I can't keep my thoughts straight. I stoke the fire until the flames crackle higher. Then I hold up the glass of water to Sayil, trying to get her to drink more water. As she takes her glass, her fingers brush against mine. She's warm to the touch, which is a good sign. But her lips are thin and chapped.

"Drink, Sayil, drink," Kamuna says and holds up her head with one hand and a glass with another. She takes a few sips on her own, but then sputters and lies back down. She's asleep in moments.

Kamuna and I stare at each other. Death holds my gaze for a breath, then says, "Find a sacrifice, if you must."

"What about Sayil?" I ask.

"What of her?"

"You will pass your mantle on to her, no?"

She doesn't reply. "Raise your daughter, Hakawati. And then we will talk." She looks at me with red-rimmed eyes. "I know this must be difficult for you, Hakawati, seeing your daughter's body hold someone else's soul."

My throat tightens, and I find myself surprised at Death's compassion.

"Shukran, Kamuna," I say, then turn away from her and Sayil, trying to keep my heart from breaking into a thousand jagged pieces.

My thoughts blur, and I try to catch onto a thread of thinking. "Kamuna," I say, glancing at the bag of clay figurines Rami left behind. "One thing. Could you bring back a figurine?"

"What for, Hakawati?"

"A sacrifice." I feel heat rise in me, a heat that flares up and threatens to consume me. But if I play this right, this fire will consume Rami, not me.

Kamuna purses her lips, then shakes her head. "No sacrifice would be willing. It won't work."

I hold Death's gaze. "Please, just try."

She sighs and holds out a palm to me.

I reach into Rami's bag and pull out a figurine.

"I am weak, Hakawati, and I can make no promises. My magic . . . the longer I stay out of death and the more rot takes over my soul seed, the less magic I have."

"Just try, I beg you."

She sighs again and runs her palm over the figurine. It's of a woman, an older woman who reminds me of my own maman. Her jaw clenches, and the figurine slowly stretches out in her palm. But it snaps back into its original size.

Kamuna closes her eyes, and I watch her chest rise and fall like a trapped animal's. The figurine stretches again, but then reverts to its original size.

"Keep trying," I tell her.

But Kamuna shakes her head.

She hands the figurine back to me. "I am sorry, Hakawati. But my magic, it's gotten too weak."

I take the figurine and smash it against the table, sending pieces of clay scattering everywhere.

Sayil whimpers and scuttles further away from me, toward my maman's chest with her smoky bottle in it.

"Move away from there, girl," I say and open the chest. I pull out my maman's bottle, and though I long to hear her voice, I set it on the table and leave her be.

"Kamuna," I say. "One last thing, then. I'll need you to let me into death."

She narrows her eyes at me. "What for, Hakawati?"

I glance at the jar on the shelf, the one holding Illyas's seed.

"I have something I need to do."

37

I FIND HIM IN THE Waiting Place, curled up in the trunk of a tree.

"Illyas," I say.

He pulls out of slumber and jumps down bleary-eyed.

"Nadine?" he says, his voice hoarse.

Something's not right with him. Or with death.

The dirt itself seems paler, more dust than earth. And the trees look sick, their branches thin, leaves brittle. I reach out to touch the tip of my finger to a tree, and it crumbles, turning to dust. A wind picks up the specks and carries them away in a swirl of black and brown.

Even the sky is shot with veins of yellows and browns, the colors of mucus, of illness. The clouds are black, rimmed with blue, like deep bruises blossoming along a leg.

"Illyas, what is it?"

"Mmm?" he says, struggling to focus his eyes on me.

"Illyas!"

He blinks a few times until he can focus on my face. But he's swaying and stumbles, catching himself onto the tree. "I feel sick," he says. "Like I'm dying all over again."

"You just need to sit," I say and watch as he slides to the ground and leans his back against the tree. I lower myself beside him, my shoulders slumped forward, watching him.

"How long has it been this way?"

"A day, two? I'm not sure. Maybe three."

I ignore the grief, the *need* I feel, seeing him like this, wanting to touch him, to comfort him.

"Illyas," I say. "Layala—I can't raise her."

His eyes snap to mine, alert now.

"What? How?"

"I tried raising her . . ."

He grunts, but then says, "My father's seed?"

I clear my throat, but force myself to look him in the eye. "It didn't work. Your father—" I try again, then clear my throat. "His soul is unusable."

"Unusable? What does that mean?"

I take a deep breath. Illyas's eyes are wide and brown and searching and pleading.

"What does it mean, Hakawati?" he asks, his voice sharp now, sharper than I've ever heard it.

I swallow hard. "It means his soul is in Jahannam and I can't use it to raise Layala."

Illyas's face breaks at this. It twists in grief, and though no tears flow, I know they would have if he were alive.

"Jahannam," he echoes, his voice cracking.

He takes a moment to understand what I just said. I watch shadows play across Illyas's face. His mouth is set in a grim line, and he doesn't look at me. "My father is in eternal suffering?" he says, almost in disbelief.

"I'm sorry, hiyati. There was nothing I could do."

Illyas sniffs, but then nods. "He was not a good person in life. Why should death reward him? He is suffering, like he made so many suffer."

I nod, reaching out to urge him closer to me. I hover my hand on Illyas's shoulder, trying to comfort him.

"I'm sorry, *habibi*, I really am."

Illyas's chin quivers, but he forces his face back into smoothness.

"I would pass him out of there if I could," I offer, "but it's beyond my reach."

230

He shakes his head. "No, I know. I don't blame you for this. But," he says, clearing his throat, "what about Layala?"

"That is the problem, hiyati. I—"

The words clog my throat, and I choke on them.

"What, Nado? What is wrong?"

"I . . . where . . . there's no one to use as Layala's sacrifice."

My eyes catch his, then glance away. "I want my baby back," I say, sputtering on my words.

Illyas gestures for me to sit closer to him. "We'll get her back."

"No matter the cost," I say. "I don't care what favor I will owe, I don't care what debt I'll have to pay."

He slumps forward, his head hanging low on his chest. "She can't stay dead," he says, so softly I strain to catch his words. He looks at me now, his eyes wide and dark and pleading. "There is nothing you can do? Nothing at all?"

I swallow, wishing upon wishes there was another way.

"Illyas," I say softly and reach out to hover my palm over his cheek. He leans in, the space between our smoky bodies feeling wider than ever.

"There has to be another way. Any other way," he says.

"There . . . is . . . could be . . . another way."

Illyas crouches before me; his eyes lock onto mine as if he's read my mind. "Then do it."

"It would mean passing—" I swallow the words back, and now my own tears flow. Illyas reaches out to brush them away, his hand ghosting through my face. "It would mean passing you to Mote, to Jahannam actually," I say. "I could use your soul seed, but it would mean—"

"It would mean I would be dead and beyond your reach."

I nod. "And . . . and what if it doesn't work? Your father, his seed . . . he's in Jahannam . . . and I know it's because of all he's done in life. All the wrong he did. And I know you haven't done that wrong. But your death was by your own hand. What if—"

Illyas stands, cutting me off. "Do it," he says. "I'm not really alive in this place." He gestures around him. "And if it can bring Layala back, I will do it again and again."

"But you're here," I argue. "And you visit us. *I* can visit *you.*" I hear the pleading, the *yearning*, in my voice, and I know Illyas does, too. He leans his face toward mine, and for a moment, just a moment, I almost feel him, so soft and strong. "And what if it is all for nothing? What if your seed does not work?"

He crouches again and hovers his hands against my cheeks. "I will always be with you, in here," he says and points to his chest, to the heart that would have been behind it if he were alive. "You know this. Layala knows this."

"I'd lose you," I splutter. "I can't—"

"I'll always be with you, in my own way."

"I don't want to lose you."

"You won't." He leans in to kiss my head, a faint touch of warmth that's not enough for me in this moment. "I knew this day would come, when I'd have to pass on anyway. It was only a matter of time. And for Layl, I'd do anything," he says in a soft voice, more a murmur.

"I'll miss you." *And I'll grieve for you until my dying breath and beyond.*

"I'll miss you, too. And Layl. You'll tell her for me, won't you? That I love her and miss her."

"You should tell her," I say. "Where is she, anyway? I expected her to be with you."

"She said to leave her alone," he says, his voice low. "So I did."

I nod, then say, "She won't agree, you know. To let you sacrifice yourself for her."

Illyas gives a dry laugh. "She won't have a choice. I am her father, and I am deciding this for her."

"I . . . maybe there's another way, or maybe I could . . ." But my voice falters. I can't think of another way.

"It's my time to go, Nado," Illyas says. He watches me with the softest look I remember seeing on his face.

"Jahannam," I say in between sniffles. "Eternal suffering."

"Maybe I won't end up there, hiyati. Maybe, maybe the good I did in life will protect me."

I nod, not trusting myself to speak. *Those who have been slain by their own hands end up in Jahannam. You know this, I know this.*

"I will find a way to get you into Mote, so you do not suffer eternity."

Illyas bows his head, but says nothing.

He reaches out a hand to me, holding it near mine. "I love you, hiyati."

I hover my hand over his, pretending I feel him. "I love you, too, hiyati."

But it's too much. Too fast.

"I can't do this," I sob. "I can't live my life alone." I sniff. "I'm being selfish, I know, raising Layl, sacrificing you. But I can't, not alone." I glance at him. "Maybe I shouldn't give you up. Perhaps, perhaps Kamuna was right, and it's Layl's time." But the words sear through my heart and I'm shaking my head, shivering in my grief. "I can't do this alone, Illyas."

He presses himself as close to me as he can without going through me. "A shared cost is no burden," he says. "And I'll share whatever that burden is, as long as we're together."

"I know," I say. And I believe it. "But perhaps, this is my cost to bear and to bear it alone."

"Hakawati," Illyas says. "Your job in life is to pass the dead through Mote. And that is what you will do."

"To pass the dead through Mote," I repeat. "Not to raise the dead."

"This is our Layl, Hakawati, our child who is dead. You are her mother, and that is your job, to keep her safe and keep her life hers. You will do what you must, Hakawati, no matter the cost."

I nod, and I stare at him until my eyes blur. "Oh, Illyas," I say. "What will I do without you?"

He smiles gently, and his eyes crinkle the way they always did in life. "What you have been doing all these years. Living a life."

We sit side by side, Illyas and I, until I know it's time to leave. My soul is drained, being in death so long, and I know the longer I stay, the harder it will be to return to life.

"You should go," he says softly. "Go home."

You are my home, I want to say. *You and Layala.*

I don't want to, but I force myself to rise. "You are my one and true love, Illyas, and you will always be."

"I know, Hakawati. You are hiyati. My life and my heart and the greatest piece of my soul. You and Layl."

I swallow the grief threatening to overwhelm me. "Then this is goodbye."

Illyas's smile is sad, but he gets to his feet and stands before me. He bows his head over mine, for just a breath. Then he pulls back.

"Goodbye, Nadine."

38

I'M SOBBING ON MY KNEES in the cemetery when I return to life. I want to curl up on top of the grave and die, just to be back in death with Illyas.

You could be with them both. You won't have to pass Illyas. And Layala, maybe, maybe she could become Death, and be able to leave the realm. Have a semblance of a life."

No!

No! That is no kind of life. That is a shadow of a life, and not one lived.

I push aside my grief, swallow the pain building in my heart. And I walk back to my home, walk back to my child, dead under my roof.

Kamuna is still there, watching Sayil in Layala's body as she eats and drinks and shivers, even though she is sitting beside the roaring fire.

"Hakawati," Death says when I shut the door behind me. "Did you do what it was you had to?"

I nod and move to the shelf with Illyas's jar.

"Hakawati?" Kamuna says, uncertain, eyeing me.

I meet her gaze. "I will sacrifice Illyas and raise Layala with his soul."

She doesn't say anything, but I notice she pulls Sayil in closer to her side. Sayil, who looks like my Layl but has none of her soul.

You are doing the right thing as her mother. You are giving her a life, the one she should live. That is your duty as her mother and your right as Hakawati.

"Nadine," Kamuna says, pulling me from my thoughts. "I know what he means to you."

"Do you?" I snap, my voice sounding far too bitter, even to me.

"Yes. And I wish it could be different."

"And there is no other way, Death? No sacrifice you can conjure?"

"No. And truly, I am sorry for your loss. I know how painful it must be."

I swallow the bile rising in my throat. "There is none who owe you a favor, who could be a sacrifice?"

Kamuna shakes her head. "If there were, I would have called in that debt many moons ago to raise my Sayil. I am sorry, Hakawati. I cannot help you."

I bow my head and hold Illyas's jar. His soul is so red, so purely red, it looks more like the color of blood than anything else. *The color of life.*

A soft hand settles on my shoulder. "I will be here, Hakawati, if you need me." She glances at Rami's body, still lying there on the ground.

I glance up at Death, her face so mournful, her eyes shining bright with tears.

"Bury him," I say.

I leave the cottage and gather more clay, more water, and everything else I need for Layl's raising. I prepare her body as I did before, and I kneel beside her. Kamuna and Sayil's eyes burn against my back, but I ignore them. Illyas's jar and Layala's seed are beside me.

"I am sorry, hiyati," I murmur.

Then I open the jar, and I eat Illyas's soul seed.

39

I FEEL PEACE.

My body feels weightless, and my heart is almost light. As if the burden I carry in my bones has been lifted by an unseen hand. I feel almost . . . happy? Nostalgic, but happy.

Illyas's story smells of him, like the earth and water, the sun and skin.

I am crying as his story runs through me, the tug in my mind of his soul's tale. I'm aching, aching, to hold him one last time.

My magic captures it, and though I want to wrench my heart from my chest, as light as it may feel now, I swallow my pain, and I tell his story.

A lonely woodcutter sat in the stump of a tree he'd just cut down. The tree was crying, or so it seemed, thin lines of sticky sap flowing out of it. But the woodcutter didn't seem to take notice, for in his hand was a long piece of bark-covered wood, hewn from a branch of the fallen tree.

The woodcutter went home that night to an empty cabin he'd built with his hands so many years before. He set that log on top of the fireplace while he made a stew for his supper. Just as the flames were dying, he took the log, about to throw it into the flames. But something in his gut told him not to.

Instead, he picked up his little carving knife and started creating notches in the wood, a notch each for the eyes, two pricks for the nose, and a little slash for the mouth.

The woodcutter began to yawn and so he set the wood down and slipped into his little cot for the night.

When he woke the next day, he slipped outside into the chill of an early morning and went to work cutting up the tree he had felled the day before.

Again, something in his gut told him to set aside a thin branch and take it home with him. That night after his supper, he cut the branch into four pieces. He then added new notches to the wood he'd already made a face for, this time creating little indents where the shoulders and legs would be. He measured everything exactly except for the right leg, which was just a bit more gnarled and a bit shorter than the left.

The next morning, the woodcutter set about his work, but just as he was heading home for the evening, he kneeled by a river to take a drink. His knees settled into the soft clay of the riverbank and some instinct told him to take a bit of that clay home. So he did.

After his supper, he molded the clay around the arms and legs he'd cut. Then he went to bed.

In the morning, the man slid the wood with legs and arms into his pocket and went about his work. As he settled in for his midday meal, he brought out the little figure and set it aside.

As the woodcutter was eating, a bird fell down beside him, its wing broken. The man cupped the little bird in his hands and, the wooden figure forgotten, took the creature home to care for it.

Weeks passed and the bird healed with the woodcutter's care.

One morning, the woodcutter said to the little bird, "I must let you go now, little friend. You have been good to me, but I must let you go back to your life."

So, the woodcutter opened his door and set the bird free.

The bird came to love the woodcutter's gentle nature and went to the riverbank where he knew he had forgotten the wooden figure.

The bird, in the language of the woods, said to the river, "Please, river, bring this figure to life for the woodcutter to have a friend of his own."

The river said, "What did that woodcutter do to deserve this, for what you ask of me is no small thing."

The bird replied, "He healed me and fed me and cared for me, asking for nothing in return."

"I see," said the river, who spoke to the tree that was felled by the woodcutter and asked if it would give its spirit to the figure. The tree, no longer a tree but cut into so many pieces, agreed, then brought the wooden figure to life.

The figure's legs grew longer and wider, and so did his arms. His face grew brighter and more cheerful, and the bark softened into skin. Leaves became hair and hands, and feet grew.

"Go be alive," said the river.

And the figure, now a man, sat up and, on feet and legs as a newborn colt does, found his way to the woodcutter's cabin.

The woodcutter was settling into his supper when he heard a knock. He opened the door to find a man standing outside.

"Come in and share my supper with me," the woodcutter said, and the man stepped in, his right leg a bit shorter than his left.

"Where do you come from?" asked the woodcutter.

"From the river, I think."

"What is your name?" asked the woodcutter.

"I don't have one, I think."

"Who is your family?" asked the woodcutter.

"The birds and the river, the trees and the woods."

And the woodcutter knew the man was the wooden figure he'd carved and put together with branches and clay.

"You may stay with me," said the woodcutter, "if you wish. I will teach you my trade and perhaps we can be friends."

The man smiled and nodded. "Yes, I'd like that."

"You will need a name," said the woodcutter.

"Shajar," said the man, "for the tree that gave me its spirit."

"Shajar," repeated the woodcutter, nodding. "And I am Ard, for the earth that gave the tree its life."

Shajar and Ard lived together for many years, and Shajar taught Ard the best way to respect old trees who were coming to the end of their lives. Ard learned how to gently pass on tree spirits, while Shajar learned how to hold a tree until it cried no more and gave up its spirit to the young trees just taking root.

When Shajar died, Arrd buried him near the stump of the tree that had given up his spirit for him. And when Shajar was shrouded with the earth that he had been born from, Arrd laid down beside his old friend and died.

40

I STARE DOWN AT SAYIL's lifeless body while I cup Layala's seed in my palm.

I kneel over her body, trying to find any resemblance she might have to Layala, but though I thought they shared something, I no longer do. The girls are like night and day. Where Layala's features are strong and dark, her brows bold, her hair a wild mass of dark curls, Sayil is light. Her skin is alabaster, her hair more the color of copper than coal. I resist the urge to lift an eyelid and see what color her eyes are.

"You are not my Layl," I whisper. "But you will be her soul's vessel. And with that, I will have to live."

Then I eat my child's soul seed.

A flower grew in a field of grass, and it stood taller and thicker than anything around her, save for the trees. The grasses, plain and green and slim, made fun of the flower for her tall stem and colorful petals.

"You have a strange head," they told her, laughing, "So many petals and so many colors. Why, we have just one head and one color and that is enough for us."

The flower would bend in the wind and rain and would try to shrivel up against the grasses, just so she wouldn't tower over them. But with each passing day of sun and rain, she grew and grew, until her stem was as thick as twenty grass blades and her flowered face was as wide as a person's fist.

The flower was miserable, for even though every person who passed by her stopped to remark on her beauty, she didn't fit in with the grass.

One day, a girl and her friend were running through the field, and they came upon the flower.

"Oh, how beautiful!" they exclaimed, dancing around the flower that stood as tall as they did. "We should take it home! We would win the town prize for prettiest plant!"

And that is what they did. They cut the flower at her feet, and she bled and cried at the pain of it all. They wrapped her in cloth and suffocated her, carrying her all the way home.

There, the girls planted the flower in a pot of soil, and they fed her with water from their well. The flower stood as tall and proud as she could, but she felt lonely without her grasses and even missed their teasing.

Even so, everyone who saw her admired her and claimed she was the prettiest flower they ever saw.

The day of the town fair came, and the girls won the prize for prettiest plant. With their blue ribbon attached to her, the flower gazed upon the sea of faces who walked by, staring for but a second or two before going on their way.

As the weeks passed by, the flower grew weaker. Her leaves shriveled, her petals fell, and the girls no longer bothered to water her. The flower was the most miserable she'd ever been.

A bird noticed her plight and came over to her.

"I can help you," the bird said. "Just give me some of your seeds, and I will plant you somewhere else."

"But then I won't be me," the flower said. "My seeds are part of me, but they're not me."

"If you don't give me your seeds, then you and your kind will die. You are already dying, so let me help you."

The flower thought for a moment, then bent her head to the bird. The bird pecked and pecked at her until it stole some of her seeds and flew off. True to its word, the bird scattered the seeds among the grasses so that many flowers grew tall and beautiful. The bird and its friends took more seeds, scattering them far and wide, until the entire field was covered in these flowers.

People would come by and take walks through the field, admiring the flowers and trampling the grass as they did so. And though our mother flower died, her kind lived on because of her.

"Oh Layl," I say, and then I'm crying. "My beautiful Layala." *Have I done this to her? Have I made her feel like that flower?*

My head feels too heavy, and I let it hang against my chest. "I'm so sorry you felt this way, Layl. I'm so sorry I didn't realize."

I want nothing more than to hold my child again, and to tell her, to tell her she is beautiful and doesn't have to sacrifice herself to be worthy. That she is worth more than gold already, simply being *her.*

But mostly, I want to tell her I'm sorry for forcing her into a pot, just like that flower.

There is nothing more to do but to wait. But I don't move.

I run my fingers along the wood of the floor, feeling how solid it is. I close my eyes and breathe in deeply, inhaling the scent of spiced bread, warm tea, and . . . us. Layala and me. I imagine Illyas's scent is lingering in the air, mixing with ours.

My eyes trace the curve of my pot-bellied stove, the one I've boiled so many pots of tea and coffee over. The clay oven in the corner, where I've baked bread for my child and fed her all these years. The floor, covered in carpets made of fibers twisted by my maman's, and her maman's hands, each one colored and layered over the other.

I turn to look at Sayil, who still hasn't uttered a word to me. I want to hear Layala's voice, even if the words are Sayil's, but the girl won't even look me in the eye, only burrows herself into her mother's side.

"I know this is not the time," Kamuna says. "But there is still the matter of passing on my mantle."

"I have lost my love today, and I am raising my child in another's body. This is not the time; you're right."

"With Sayil alive," Kamuna continues, "and Layala, well, yet to be raised—but I have no doubt she will be—I will need to decide what to do."

"You have your child," I say. "You have her to pass the mantle to. Just as we discussed with Rami."

Kamuna glances down at Sayil. "But she is so *alive.*"

"She is in another's body. *My daughter's* body."

"She is alive, Hakawati. I—" Death bows her head. "I remember now what it feels like to truly mourn. To mourn not the dead, but the living."

"You don't want to send her back into death," I say softly, understanding what she is saying. I feel so tired, and though I want to argue, I don't.

Kamuna shakes her head. "This is *life*, Hakawati. *Life.* And she is here, alive."

I glance at Sayil's body, still showing no signs of life.

"When Layala returns, what will you do?" I ask. "Because I will kill you myself if you lay a finger on her."

"I don't know, Hakawati. I really don't. But I know I am dying, and someone has to take my place."

"Well, it won't be my daughter," I say. "So, it will have to be yours."

Kamuna is hunched over, I realize now, her skin gray. Sayil is staring at her mother, but her eyes look blank. As if she is neither here nor elsewhere, as if being in death for so long has robbed her body of being able to hold life, no matter the seed in her.

"I'm dying," Kamuna says again. "My magic is weak. Even with a sacrifice, I wouldn't be able to raise a fruit fly from the dead. I don't think I can even return to death easily. And I feel . . ."

But I don't wait to hear how Kamuna feels. I turn my back to both Death and her child and stare at Sayil's body, waiting for my own child to return to life.

41

"You should rest," Kamuna says. I'm nodding off before the dying fire.

"She hasn't come back yet," I say, but I let Death lead me to my cot.

"Rest," she insists. "I will wake you up if she so much as stirs an eyelash."

I let her tuck my blanket around me and, as I listen to her putter around my kitchen, I fall into a fitful sleep.

"Hakawati," I hear someone saying, pulling me out of a nightmare. "Wake up."

"Mmm?" I say, then realize it's Kamuna speaking.

"Layala!" I yell and jump out of my cot.

Sayil's body is standing there, before the fire, staring at me with eyes so bright and blue, they rival the brightest morning sky.

And holding a knife to her throat is a ghoul.

42

"MAMAN!" LAYALA SCREAMS WITH SAYIL'S voice. She's watching me with wide, wild eyes, but they're not my baby's eyes. They're not Layala's deep, dark eyes.

My heart wrenches in two, but I lunge for the ghoul, who pulls Layala out of my reach.

Sayil is crouching behind her mother, who is staring at another woman.

I recognize her, the twigs in her hair and the clay-color of her skin. "Earth," I say. "What are you doing in my home?"

"Jinn," she says with a sneer. "Foolish little jinn who doesn't know when to let things alone."

"Get out, Earth," I say, but my voice is weak, and I'm trembling. "Get out of my home and take your ghouls and golems with you."

I count two more ghouls and one golem crowding my cottage. I don't doubt there are more outside.

"Where is my son, jinn?" Earth demands. "He was here. I can smell it."

"He left."

"Liar!"

She snaps her fingers at a golem, who rushes forward, holding a sack in his hand. There's something inside, and I hear the rustling of wings.

"This belongs to you, I believe," Earth says and snaps her fingers again.

The golem reaches in and pulls out a struggling Saqr by the neck.

"You are not the only one with clay magic, jinn," Earth says. "I sent your little bewitched bird to check up on my son. And what do I learn but that he has come to *you*, and you stupidly killed him. Here, in the very spot I stand."

I try to swallow but my mouth is dry, so dry I choke.

The golem flings Saqr at me, and when he lands at my feet, he shatters into more clay shards than I can count.

"An eye for an eye, jinn," Earth says. "A child for a child."

She jerks her chin at the ghoul holding a knife to Layala's throat.

"No!" I scream and grab for the ghoul's arm. I hurl him back, and just as I do, a golem grabs Layala.

But my girl fights. She kicks at the creature, then bites his arm. He yelps and pulls back, and Layala skirts over to me.

"Behind me," I tell her, but she doesn't listen. Instead, she kicks the ghoul and shoves him toward the fire.

I reach for the knife he'd wielded and hold it out in front of me.

"Oh, jinn," Earth says. "One little blade won't do a thing."

Her skin hardens into bark, but she can still move. She gestures at the two other ghouls, but Kamuna steps before them and stops them in their tracks. They stare up at her, and just as one reaches out for Kamuna, she kicks him back. He stumbles, clutching his abdomen and gasping for breath.

Layala is struggling with the third ghoul, but as she fights him off, I reach out behind him and press my finger to the back of his head. He turns into clay, and I kick the figurine into the fire.

"Layl!" I scream just as a golem drags her back.

I whip the blade at the golem and manage to nick him in the arm. But he doesn't let go of Layl.

I jump toward her, then push the golem out of the way. But before I can press my finger to his head, he runs for the door and jumps outside.

"Worthless!" Earth shouts, but she comes toward me.

"No!" Kamuna yells, and shoves herself in front of me. "Your war is with me. It has always been."

But I've already shoved Layala back and am urging her and Sayil out through the roof.

The two ghouls reach for Kamuna, and she lets them kick her to her knees.

"Go!" I yell at the girls, but they don't obey.

Sayil pushes me out of the way and runs toward her mother, who is kneeling before Earth.

"Leave her be!" Sayil screams, and her voice is Layala's voice. Her face, screwed up in anger, is Layala's.

I turn to Layala, in Sayil's body, and I urge her up to the roof. But she won't move.

"No, maman," she says. "This has to end here."

"Earth!" Layala yells, and she pushes past me. "It's me you want."

I pull Layala's arm and shove her back, but Earth has her eyes on my child.

"I don't understand," Earth says. "That one protects you, jinn," she says, eyeing Layala in Sayil's skin. "But this one protects Death," she adds, eyeing Sayil in Layala's body.

She snaps her fingers at the two ghouls.

Kamuna turns to glance at me, and something passes between us.

Her body coils, and I feel mine following suit.

The ghouls move toward our girls, and like snakes disturbed from our nests, we strike.

I fight the one whose eyes are set on Layala. He doesn't even realize I'm on him until my weight is pressing him to the ground.

I elbow him in the throat, and he makes a gurgling sound as he tries to push me off with his hip. But I press my knee deep into the soft spot in his abdomen, just under his heart, and he howls in pain.

"You. Will. Not. Harm. My. Child," I say, and before he can throw my weight off him, he is clay.

Earth is moving toward the door, but Kamuna blocks her way. The other ghoul, I notice, is lying still on the ground. I don't see the injury Kamuna inflicted, but I know he is dead.

Layala and Sayil stand beside each other, seeming more like sisters than strangers in each other's skins.

"Leave," Kamuna says to Earth, who seems more like skin than bark now. She appears shorter, too, more like sapling than oak tree.

"You are weak, Death," Earth says. "Your time has come. I can feel it. Your realm, and everything in it, will be mine."

"Leave," Kamuna repeats. "Outside of death, you are as weak as a fistful of dirt without those ghouls and golems by your side."

"You will see," Earth says. "You will see what happens when you anger Mother Earth, when you kill her only son."

"Just go," I say, the tiredness in my voice thick. "You never cared for him in life."

Earth purses her lips. "But he was *mine*." She holds my gaze. "I will go," Earth says, "but I will return."

Kamuna slams the door behind her. I move to lock it, then turn to the girls.

"Tea?" I say, then laugh at the absurdity of my offer.

We're all laughing now, buckling over and letting ourselves drop to the ground.

I reach for Layala, who leans in for a hug. Her smell is not her own, but her touch is.

"Maman," she says, pulling back from me, though she still clutches my arms. "What about the mantle, maman?" She glances in Kamuna's direction.

But I shake my head. "Not now, Layl. Please."

43

WE SIT, THE FOUR OF US, sipping tea that has now grown cold. I have told Layala about Illyas, and we've all been silent ever since.

"My mantle," Kamuna says, and her skin is more gray, more ashen, than even a few minutes ago. "I need to pass it."

"I will do it," Layala says just as Sayil says, "It is my duty."

The girls look at each other, and something passes between them.

"No, Layl," I say. "I brought you back, I sacrificed your *father*."

Layala meets my gaze. "I will bring him back."

"He's in Jahannam, Layl. There's no bringing him back."

"When I am Death, my magic—"

"There's no *when*, Layl! I forbid it."

She tilts her head and, though her eyes are Sayil's blue, there's something of Layala's steel stubbornness in them.

"No, Layl," I repeat.

But she turns to Sayil, ignoring me.

"We will both do it," she says, and Sayil nods.

"I don't want to leave my body," Sayil says. "And it is my duty to take the mantle."

"I refuse to have my father suffer in Jahannam for all eternity," Layala says, then adds, "I am sorry, maman."

I set down my tea and slump in my chair.

Kamuna turns to me. "My mantle must pass, one way or another."

"Your daughter knows it is her duty—"

"And yours knows it is her privilege," Kamuna cuts in.

We stare at each other for a few breaths. "You can pass your mantle to only one."

"Actually, I can pass it to both."

I blink. I feel a soft hand on mine and look down at it. Layala, but the hand is wrong. It's not hers.

"Maman," she says with Sayil's voice, and my heart breaks. Layala is *alive*, but she is not her. She doesn't sound or smell or look like my Layl.

I slip my hand away and tuck it in my lap.

My breath shudders, then I say, "I love you, Layala, enough to let you go."

She looks at me with wide blue eyes and smiles. "Shukran, maman. I know this is hard for you. It is for me, too. But, but now I can save baba. And I can save death itself."

"You will visit," I say.

"Always, maman."

"And I will visit you."

Layala smiles and nods.

She takes Sayil's hand in her own, and the two of them, though night and day, look to be the other's half.

Kamuna reaches both her hands out to the girls. "Shukran," she says. "You will have each other, and that is more than I could have ever hoped for myself. To have another to share the burden with."

The girls look at each other and grin. "I never had a sister," Sayil says.

Layala's eyes glimmer. "Neither have I."

Kamuna turns to me, a sad smile on her face. "It was always their time, Hakawati. Our interference could never change that."

And though I'm in pain, though I feel my own soul splintering into pieces, I smile. *Layala is happy.*

I think of the prayer beads, of the wish-prayer I have spoken since before her birth, when she was still in my womb.

Keep her safe.
Keep her happy.
Let her find good love.
Let her know peace.
Let her know her heart and mind.
Let her be.

Let her be, I think.
And so, I do.

44

KAMUNA SETTLES DOWN IN THE cemetery behind my cottage, Layala and Sayil on either side.

"It is my time," she says. "I have no grief, no mourning," she insists, more to herself. She takes the girls' hands, then turns to me.

I lean in to Layala and hug her tight. Then I reach for Sayil, who gives my hand a warm squeeze.

"I will die, but you must not tell my story, Hakawati," Kamuna says. "Preserve my soul seed, so I can remain tethered to death, to the Waiting Place."

I bow my head, but then nod in agreement.

Kamuna stretches out over the soil and leans her head back. She sinks into the earth, and I watch her body relax.

"Come, rest your heads beside me," she tells the girls.

I'm crying, but I try not to sob as I watch both Layala and Sayil lie down on either side of Death, resisting the urge to yank my daughter out of Kamuna's grasp.

My baby, my Layala. My whole heart and soul.

Kamuna's breathing tapers, and I witness the moment her chest no longer rises.

I choke back a sob as Layala's and Sayil's bodies grow still.

Keep her safe.

Keep her happy.

Let her find good love.

Let her know peace.

Let her know her heart and mind.

Let her be.

I lean toward Kamuna's body and there, lying in the soil, is a pomegranate seed.

Layala's and Sayil's aren't here, though. Theirs have gone to become part of death itself, like Kamuna's once was.

Keep them safe.

Keep them happy.

Let them find good love.

Let them know peace.

Let them know their hearts and minds.

Let them be.

I pocket Kamuna's soul seed, and with the shovel from the shed behind my home, I start digging three graves.

45

THE NEXT MORNING, THE FRONT of my cottage is littered with crimson seeds. I hoist my basket and start filling it with the seeds. Then, with the basket as heavy as my heart, I settle inside my empty home and start telling the stories of the dead, just like I've always done, and just like I'll do until my dying breath.

46

A month later.

Kamuna lingers in death, but as a soul now. She's been watching over our girls, and every morning, she visits me, just as Illyas once did. She still has a bit of her old power, but it's pale, like tea leaves strained too many times.

She tells me about Layala and Sayil, of their magic growing. The two of them, each complementing the other.

Layala visited me once, only for a minute. Her magic, though it's gaining strength, is still too weak to allow her to stay longer. But I visit her every day in death. She is so happy, her face so radiant, her smile brighter than I've seen it in such a long time.

"There is so much to learn and explore here, maman!"

I don't say, *You could have said the same in life.* Instead, I smile at my daughter and try not to think about how blue her eyes are and how they should be dark as the night sky. Their souls look like the bodies they were threaded into when they were raised, not like their original skins. It's happened before, I know, when souls take on the color and shape of their new bodies, but it's jarring, though I'm grateful Layala is alive. No matter what skin her soul has taken on.

Sayil has warmed up to me and comes running when I visit, throwing her long arms around my neck to hug me.

"Hakawati," she says, then spills into a long tale about how her day went since I last saw her, which was yesterday.

I'm feeling lighter, seeing my daughter and Sayil, who's become her sister, so happy.

Every time I see Layala, she offers me the same promise, though I never ask it of her. "I will find baba, and I will bring him back."

"I know you will, Layala," I lie. "I know you will."

I offer her a plucked flower, a white one, with edges limned in brown, a few of the petals yellowing. She cups it in her hands, and the flower blooms to life, brown melding into white. She smiles at me, her smile so like Illyas's I can't breathe, even with the wrong skin she wears. But I smile back at my child, at Death, and I think, *let her be happy, let her be safe. Let her be.*

Back in life, I'm alone in my cottage. I don't go into town unless I need something, as I always have. Except this time, I don't have Illyas's visits to look forward to, and I don't have Layala around.

I do have maman, though I don't bring her out much. She tires too easily, and I feel bad forcing her out of her slumber.

Instead, I make sure Kamuna's soul seed is safe in a jar of holding water, tucked away on my shelf, where I look at it every day.

I'm passing souls along, like I did before.

But the days stretch on before me, and I decide, for the first time in years, to make a visit deep into the woods.

The woods are dark and deep, and sunlight doesn't cut through the thick canopy of leaves and branches above me. The air smells of sweet rot, of leaves and dirt and rainwater. The leaves rustle, and tree branches creak as a breeze stirs through.

Animals scurrying by are shadowy figures, and every tree root could be a snake in this dark.

It's been a while, years really. But my feet know the way still.

Time has shifted the once-familiar earth, and where there were natural landmarks, they are moved or gone altogether. The stone I thought would be before me is really to my right. And where I thought the great tree with the exposed trunk stood is shifted to my left, the little bark left on it clawed into ribbons by animals.

Still, I am greeting the landmarks, one by one, like old sentries posted at city gates: the nest of rocks that always seemed to me to be the jagged teeth of a slain giant, the tree trunk strangled with thick vines.

The path ends abruptly at a cabin built of hewn logs, leaves, vines, and moss. It looks as if it's been molded out of the dirt and trees themselves. The air is heavy with the scent of rotted leaves, and I hear moving water nearby. I learned from Kamuna that part of death's river, the part that leads right to Nahr, flows through this part of the woods.

I owe the river witch a visit.

Death is the same as ever, just as gray and dull as when I left it not even a full day before. I find the boat I used before and float down the silver river, calling out for Nahr.

The river witch is lying on the riverbank, watching me with her slitted eyes.

"You've returned," she says.

"A favor for a favor," I say. "Your sister, I'll raise her now."

The river witch smiles, and her teeth don't seem as sharp as they did before. I notice for the first time her tongue is rimmed with scales and splinters of bone. "Follow me, Hakawati." She chuckles to herself. "It's good to have Death's mother on my side."

As she shoves my boat forward, she swims alongside it. "Your daughter has proven most friendly. Her and the other one." Nahr pauses for a moment. "Two Deaths," she says. "That's never been before, I don't think. At least, not in my memory."

But then she's guiding the boat down the river and toward the pond Sayil's body was buried in before. Nahr disappears under those waters, and she returns what feels like years later, carrying a body out of the pond.

The river witch's sister is made of salt and the brine of the sea. She is pale, with white dust coating her skin.

I raise her with clay from death's soil and blood from the river witch. The sacrifice was not needed, the witch being made from death itself, in a way that not even Layala was, being death-touched.

"I owe you, Hakawati," Brine says.

"You do not," Nahr says sharply. "She owed me a favor, and she has now repaid it. You owe her nothing."

But Brine bows her head to me anyway.

"We will avenge you," Brine says. "As we will ourselves. For Earth did this to us."

I've told both witches my story, and they have told me theirs. We've had hours in death, together, and all three of our stories have converged onto betrayal by Earth.

"I will hold you to that," I say.

"As Hakawati or as Death's mother?" Nahr asks.

"Both, neither," I say, confused by what I feel. "As a woman," I say finally.

The two sisters bow their heads at me.

"We have a third Sister," Brine says, "who spends her time on a mountain, in a nest. She will help us, for Earth smote her, too."

"We have a fourth Sister," Nahr says, but her nose is wrinkled. "She will not help, perhaps, but—"

"We will convince her," Brine interrupts. "Leave her to me. I am her favorite."

"I will leave you now," I say. And since I'm already in death, I find Layala and Sayil, just for a few minutes.

They're happy, smiling about some new piece of magic they've realized they have.

"Maman!" Layala calls, beaming at me. "I was able to fashion a *marid* out of river water and clay!"

A river witch, I think. And my mind goes to Nahr and Brine, wondering who fashioned them.

"And I was able to create a roc out of a piece of the sky and some feathers I found," Sayil says, stretching out her arm to the heavens. A large bird, with a beak like a hawk's and eyes as golden as the sun, latches onto Sayil's arm with claws as long as fingers.

I smile at them, and though it pains me to leave my daughter behind, I return to my life, to my cottage, and to my day.

Keep them safe.

Keep them happy.

Let them find good love.

Let them know peace.

Let them know their hearts and minds.

Let them be.

I count out each wish-prayer on a bead and repeat each one until the words have blurred together and I no longer can make them out.

The next morning, I step outside my door to a ground filled with so many red seeds, I need two baskets to carry them all inside.

I am Hakawati. My job is to tell the stories of the dead, to pass them along to Mote.

And this is what I do, with my basket on my hip, and stories to tell settling sweet on my tongue.

Acknowledgments

IN WRITING THIS BOOK, I learned I had more community and support behind me than I could have ever imagined. To everyone who found ways to celebrate me and this book, shukran, truly.

I could not have written a folkloric story if not for my baba, who raised me on a steady diet of oral tradition, and fed my soul with Arabic. Shukran for his patient love and education. My mother, with her unwavering pride and support and love: I may not say it, but I appreciate you more than you know.

To my family, who have been even more excited than me for this: you make me feel supported, especially Tita Lily, Aunty Joanne, Uncle Tony, Aunty Alison, Aunty Judy, Aunty Jackie, and everyone else. Blood is everything.

To my husband, for listening to my half-cooked tales before I've even written them down. You're my rock.

Shukran to all my teachers who fed my hunger for books and learning in my formative years, especially Ms. Oleszczuk and Mr. Mcdermott.

My friends, you all know who you are, have supported me so much, and I can't tell you how much that means to me. Kee, Shal, Ashley, Nicole, Sevde, you're the best. Mercy, you're an amazing friend, person, and beta reader, whose constant support, intelligence, and creativity I simply could not live without. And thank you to everyone else who has been so excited for me: Olivia, Desiree, Rianne, Kaitlyn L., Anna(s), I have felt so supported by you.

To everyone else not named, but still seen.

My wonderful, hardworking, and intelligent agent, Kaitlyn Katsoupis: I would not be here without you. Shukran.

Thanks to Hoopoe, especially Nadine and Sue, for believing in me and my story.

Last but not least, I thank all the writers whose books I've read and who shaped my mind and thoughts. It takes a village of both the living and the dead to mold a mind.

Printed in the USA
CPSIA information can be obtained
at www.ICGtesting.com
JSHW080855060324
58611JS00002B/2